Investigating the Heart
By Heidi Renee Mason

Dedication

This book is dedicated to my husband, Cameron, and my daughters, Chloe, Sophie, and Averi. You are my very reason for existence.

Prologue

Moving as quickly as a woman seven months pregnant was capable of, Emma McCoy headed to the front door of her house. The loud knocking had awakened her from her afternoon nap. Emma yawned, trying to appear awake. She didn't remember being this exhausted during her other pregnancies. This time, she could barely stay awake during the day.

"I'll be right there!" She called toward the general direction of the front door.

She wondered to herself who it could be. Her best friend, Sadie, never knocked, and her husband, Jacob, was out of town on business. Mom and Dad wouldn't have bothered knocking. They would have known she would probably be napping while the girls napped.

Opening the front door, she saw the two policemen. Fear immediately crept up inside of her chest. Her first thought upon seeing the officers was that something was wrong with her parents. Had they been hurt? Emma prayed the policemen were at the wrong address, but she had a feeling deep inside of her gut that they were not.

"Can I help you?" Her heart raced inside of her chest. She willed herself to stay calm.

"Mrs. McCoy," said the male officer. "Can we come inside, please?"

"Of course." Emma led them through the dining room and into her living room. She offered the officers a seat, but instead of sitting herself, she paced the living room floor, panic rising in spite of her best efforts to keep it in check. "Someone please tell me what's going on. Has there been some kind of accident? Is someone hurt?"

"Mrs. McCoy, please sit down," said the female officer. "We need you to stay calm. Since you're pregnant, we can't have you getting too upset."

Emma sat down awkwardly in the rocking chair.

The antique rocker had been in her family for generations. Her parents had given it to her as a gift when she gave birth to her oldest daughter. She ran her hands across the aged wood, thinking absently of her children, who were upstairs napping. She was aware that her palms were sweating and her heart was racing. She tried to slow her breathing, but she felt like she might throw up.

"Someone please tell me what's wrong. I know something is wrong," she said impatiently, looking directly at the officers for answers. "Is it my parents?"

"Mrs. McCoy, there has been an accident. Your husband's plane went down while it was descending into Canada. They searched, but there were no survivors," said the female officer as she looked intently at Emma. "I am so sorry to bring you this news."

"What do you mean? There must be some mistake. Jacob's plane wasn't even flying to Canada. He was going to California on business." Emma was momentarily thankful realizing the officers must be mistaken.

"I know this is a shock, Mrs. McCoy, but it has been confirmed. The passenger on the plane to Canada was definitely your husband. We have copies of his plane ticket and his passport. We have him on the airport video surveillance. He boarded the plane with another passenger, a woman named Veronica Smith. I believe you might know her as well," said the policeman.

"Veronica is our neighbor. I thought she was going to Pennsylvania to visit her family. That's what she told me last week. Why were Jacob and Veronica on a plane together? Jacob was supposed to be going to California, not Canada. I don't understand! Why was he with Veronica?" Emma demanded as a million questions filled her mind.

She sat for a moment trying to wrap her brain around the information. The small voice which she had ignored for the past year spoke loudly in her head now. She had been suspicious of Jacob and Veronica, but told herself she was just being paranoid. Jacob had told her she was just emotional because of the pregnancy. Emma had agreed that he was probably right, and had pushed aside the nagging suspicion she felt.

Images she had ignored because she didn't want to believe them now paraded through her mind. There had been many times she had accused her husband of being friendlier with their neighbor than he should be. Jacob always got angry with her and blamed her for being paranoid. Emma always backed off, not wanting to fight with him.

In that instant, Emma's denial came crashing down on her. She saw Jacob helping the beautiful and mysterious Veronica trim the hedge between the houses. She saw them laughing together at something Jacob had said. She heard Jacob's insistence that he was "just being neighborly." Emma remembered the morning she had seen Jacob and Veronica talking quietly on the sidewalk, their familiarity with each other making her jealous. Emma had chosen to ignore all of these things, but they could not be ignored now. The room began to spin. She felt faint. Jacob had been having an affair with Veronica, and now they were both dead. What was she going to do? She was alone, with two little girls and another on the way. Emma tried to stand, but her legs wouldn't support her. The two officers rushed over and caught Emma as she slipped into oblivion.

Chapter One
Six Years Later

"Mama, it's time to get up now. Your alarm is going off," whispered six-year-old Rose.

My eyes flew open and I jumped out of bed. How had I slept through the alarm again? Luckily, Rose had climbed into bed with me sometime in the night. If she hadn't, it was hard to tell how long I would have slept.

"Thanks, Baby." I planted a quick kiss on Rose's head. "Run and wake Lily and Dahlia for me, please?"

"Sure thing Mama." Rose bounced and ran down the hall. I cringed as her voice reverberated off the walls; certain it would wake her sisters, and quite possibly the neighborhood.

Knowing I didn't have much time to get ready, I headed to the bathroom. I turned the shower on as hot as it would go. Stepping out of my pajamas, I stood under the hot water, hoping it would wash away the sleepiness I still felt. Ten minutes later, I slid my favorite faded jeans over my curvy body, and put on a black T-shirt and tennis shoes. Today, I was extra thankful for my long, wavy, strawberry blonde hair. It was one of my best assets, and the fact that it was wash and wear would come in handy. After a quick coat of mascara, and a shot of concealer to cover the dark circles under my emerald eyes, I declared that was good enough. I was a "no frills" kind of woman. I didn't have time for anything more than that.

Heading into the kitchen, I began to toast the bagels that my daughters loved. I poured three glasses of orange juice for the girls and a steaming cup of coffee for myself. I was grateful I had remembered to set the timer on the coffee pot last night. I didn't have time to wait for my caffeine infusion. I added a generous amount of creamer. I loved the kick but not necessarily the taste. In my opinion, the bitterness of black coffee needed a little help in order to be palatable. I was already thinking about getting my next cup at work. With the way my morning had started, I was going to need all the caffeine I could get today.

"Girls, fifteen minutes until the bus comes," I called upstairs. "Get down here and eat, please!"

I heard the scampering of feet on the wooden stairs. Rose was dressed in her usual eclectic clothing. Today she wore a ruffled skirt with a polka dot pattern, paired with flowered leggings and a striped shirt. Rose was a firm believer in patterns. Eight-year old Dahlia followed closely behind Rose, dressed in her "comfy clothes" as she called them. Dahlia lived in sweat pants and T-shirts. The comfortable clothing suited my middle daughter's lighthearted personality. Dahlia was my easy girl. She was helpful, and enjoyed making other people happy. She was a perpetual sunny spot in my hectic world.

"Where is Lily?" I asked.

"She's still figuring out what she's going to wear. You know every day is a fashion show for Lily," said Dahlia, rolling her eyes.

A couple of minutes later, Lily sauntered into the kitchen with the regal air of a queen. My oldest daughter had been born a miniature adult. I often worried that she was missing out on her childhood by being so serious. Lily had a difficult time with Jacob's death, and it had made her grow up too fast. Lily was not playful and carefree like her sisters. I thought she had more worries than a girl of ten should have.

"Good morning, Princess Lily," I said with a smile. "It is so good of you to join us."

"Good morning." Lily gave me her best scowl.

Lily was not a morning person. We had all learned long ago to avoid conversations with her until after lunchtime.

"Ten minutes until the bus gets here, so eat quickly, girls." They grumbled and complained as always. I gave them what they fondly called my "mom look" and they began eating. I've often wondered what my "mom look" was, but it seemed to work, so I just went with it. I'd take whatever help I could get.

Twenty minutes later, the girls were off to school, and I was left to clean up the kitchen. I loved my kitchen. It was one of my favorite rooms in the house. It's large and sunny with a huge bay window that my table sat in front of. I loved sitting there and having my coffee in the morning. In my opinion, I had the perfect kitchen.

Luckily, I didn't have a long commute to work. The coffee shop I owned, Morning Glory, was conveniently located next door. My shop manager, Jane, was extremely capable, which allowed me to have mornings at home with the girls.

"Okay, I have five minutes to myself." I sighed, taking a seat at the kitchen table. I sipped my coffee while I thought of all of the things I had to do today.

Sadly, I realized that I was already exhausted and the day hadn't even begun. Being a single mom was a lot to handle, not to mention running a business and taking care of the house. I scolded myself for whining, though. I was extremely lucky to have these things. My daughters were exhausting, but I couldn't even begin to imagine how I would have survived the last six years without them.

When Jacob died, I had to decide how I was going to spend the rest of my life. I had been a stay at home mom for years, so unfortunately I had no job history. Jacob had been the breadwinner, and much to my surprise had no insurance, which I only found out when I needed it most. I came to the harsh realization that my family had no income. Jacob made decent money, but he handled all of the finances, making me oblivious to money matters. It came as quite a shock to me that we had absolutely no savings, and quite a lot of debt. I had no choice but to sell our family home, since there was no way to continue the payments.

Thank God, my parents came to the rescue. The girls and I moved into the large, rambling Victorian house in which I had grown up. I loved my childhood home, and was more than happy to seek refuge there with my mom and dad. My parents had truly saved the day, allowing me time to give birth to Rose and figure out our future. The girls and I settled into a comfortable routine at my parents' house. There was more than enough room for all of us in the spacious home, and my daughters and I were happy to stay.

My parents were amazing. They helped me when I needed it, but didn't interfere with my parenting when I didn't want them to. My father, a property developer, made a very comfortable living, and insisted that I stay home and take care of the girls for as long as I wanted.

Two years later, my dad was trying to decide whether or not to sell the building he owned next door. I had been developing a plan in my mind for several months and I presented the idea of opening a coffee shop. My dad thought that the building would be the perfect place for one. Rose had just turned two years old, and I didn't know the first thing about running a business, but I did know that I needed a source of income. Again, my faithful father stepped in and helped me. I opened Morning Glory, my trendy little coffee shop, the following year.

It seemed that things were finally on track for me when tragedy struck again. My beloved parents were killed in a head-on crash on their way home from dinner six months after I opened Morning Glory. I remember being paralyzed with grief. I literally didn't think I was going to make it to the other side of all of the tragedy I had seen.

Like the angels that they were, my parents provided for me even after their deaths. They left the family home, paid in full, to me. I now had a place to live and a means to support my girls, all thanks to my parents.

Feeling completely alone, my world was turned on end. I had no idea how I was going to care for three small girls and manage a household and business by myself. I knew I had no choice, but the task ahead of me seemed daunting. Out of the blue, my life-long best friend, Sadie Ross, came to my rescue. Sadie moved into the upstairs apartment which was attached to my house. She and I synced our schedules, and Sadie stepped in to help me with the girls.

I had experienced my share of tragedy, but I was also aware that I had unbelievably supportive people in my life. I tried not to see the tragedies, but instead focus on the blessings. I wanted to be thankful every day for the things I still had. There was no denying that being a single mom was exhausting, though, and I definitely had bad days. I took my last sip of coffee and hoped this would not turn out to be one of them.

"Looks like my alone time is up," I sighed, rinsing out my cup. I walked out the front door and headed next door to Morning Glory.

Chapter Two

"Good morning, Jane," I said as I walked into the coffee shop. "As usual, the place looks great. I don't know what I would do without you."

"You know I love this place," said Jane happily. That's why you keep me around!"

"Mostly, I keep you around because I love you," I laughed.

Jane was thirty-five and had never been married. She was just sassy enough to be intimidating, and her blue hair and tattoos belied the fact that she was really just a kind, softhearted woman on the inside. We had become great friends, and I felt comfortable leaving the shop in her capable hands when I needed a break.

Morning Glory was busy as usual. It was hip and trendy. It could best be described as "shabby chic." The easy atmosphere attracted the young people. It also enticed the older people in town I have known my entire life. I have an extremely loyal customer base. I couldn't believe the success it had become. I thought it was pretty impressive for a woman who had no idea how to run a business! I had strongly adhered to the policy of "fake it 'til you make it." Unbelievably, it had worked.

My day included one of the parts of my job that I liked the least; I needed to work on my shop inventory. I told Jane where I was going, and headed to the stock room and got lost in the world of numbers.

I glanced at the clock, and realized I had been counting stock for an hour already. Taking a break and heading up front, I noticed all of the familiar faces. I enjoyed interacting with my customers and getting to know my regulars.

I was about to go back to counting when a new face caught my eye. My heart skipped a beat as I surveyed the stranger in the corner booth. I couldn't figure out how I had missed him before. This was a man that couldn't possibly be overlooked. Judging from his very muscular frame and long legs beneath the table, I could tell he was tall. He had raven black hair that curled over his ears and fell playfully over his forehead. He was bent over a table full of papers, nursing a cup of coffee. If I were interested in men, I would definitely be attracted to this one.

I quickly reminded myself that I was definitely not looking for a man. I had sworn off of relationships after Jacob died. The hurt and betrayal I felt when I found out about his unfaithfulness was almost more than I could bear. My marriage to Jacob had been rocky from the beginning, but I had honestly thought he respected the boundaries of the vows we made. Apparently, they made little difference to Jacob. His betrayal made me realize that I was much better off alone. I didn't think I could live through more heartbreak in this lifetime. I was startled to see the stranger stand up, bringing me back to the present. My heart began to race as I realized he was looking right at me. I had an intense feeling of connection to the man. I couldn't explain it since I had never seen him before.

He was even better looking than I originally thought, and my palms began to sweat as he headed my way. He towered over me as he approached the counter.

"Hey there, this coffee is fabulous. Could I trouble you for a refill?" said the man, his blue eyes sparkling like the ocean. It would be a strong woman who could say no to this guy.

"Of course," I responded politely, trying not to make eye contact.

I refilled the man's coffee cup and was ready to return to my inventory. This smooth operator wasn't going to sink his teeth into me.

"My name's Liam O'Reilly. I'm new in town. Is this your shop?"

"Yes." I didn't elaborate.

"Do you have a name?" he asked with a laugh.

"I'm Emma, and I need to get back to work. This place doesn't run itself."

I turned sharply, looking away from his penetrating, blue-eyed stare. I headed to the back room, suddenly needing to put some distance between myself and the stranger. From the inventory room I could see him standing there, confusion written all over his handsome face. A man like that was probably used to having women fall all over him. Well, if he had expected that reaction from me, he had another thing coming. I wasn't so easily won over by a handsome face.

I scolded myself as I stacked boxes in the storage room. What had come over me? I had certainly been rude. That wasn't like me at all. As a customer service professional, I didn't treat people that way. I couldn't figure out why the man had gotten under my skin so easily.

***

Back at his table, Liam ruffled through the papers in front of him. He had noticed Emma the minute she walked through the door. He saw her once before, six years ago when the police had gone to her house to tell her about her husband's death. He had been the FBI agent who was investigating the case of Veronica Smith and her ring of jewelry thieves. It had been the biggest case of his career, and the one that had haunted him the longest. He had been at the site of the plane crash, and had been the one who identified the bodies of Jacob and Veronica. He had flown back to Jacob and Emma's hometown of Beckland, Ohio, with the intention of breaking the news to Emma himself. When he arrived at her house, though, he had gotten sidetracked by a phone call. He remained outside, while two local police officers had broken the news to her. He had seen her open the front door, and the sight of her, nervous, pregnant, and about to get the worst news of her life had stayed with him the past six years. He couldn't get the image of her out of his head. Seeing her today brought it all back to him, along with a new feeling of intense desire.

Liam knew Jacob and Veronica were headed into Canada, and he was there waiting for them. The plane crash had been purely coincidental. He remembered his frustration. He was so close to cracking the case. Over the last six years, he had worked tirelessly; in fact, it became his life's obsession, to find where Veronica had stashed the fortune of stolen jewels. Recently, he even bought the house that Veronica owned, hoping to find some clue leading him to the jewels. More than anything, Liam wanted answers. He had never been so determined to close a case before. He had bought Veronica's house and had come to Beckland hoping to learn more about Jacob and Veronica's illegal activities. He hoped that if he got to know Emma a little better he might glean some useful information about her late husband. He looked toward the back room where Emma had disappeared, hoping to catch another glimpse of her. She was stunning. It certainly wouldn't be a hardship to become friends with her.

He had a full day of work ahead of him. He would come back tomorrow, have some coffee and hopefully make friends with Emma, and learn more about Jacob. Liam had forgotten how beautiful she was. He needed to be very sure he kept his head in the game. He couldn't afford to become distracted by her. Gathering his belongings, he headed out the front door.

***

I walked back to the front of the shop, and noticed that Liam was gone. I would have to apologize for my rudeness if I ever saw him again. What was it about him that set me on edge?

As much as I hated inventory, I was lost in my work when Sadie sauntered into Morning Glory. Sadie came in each day during her lunch break. She was a research librarian at the public library down the street. She was tall and thin, and had waist-length honey-blonde hair that looked like spun gold. She was the most beautiful woman I had ever seen, and anyone who saw her would agree. If she hadn't been so genuinely sweet, it would have been very easy to hate her.

Growing up, it had been difficult to get the attention of any boy when Sadie was with me. She generally had a line of admirers a mile long because she was too nice to tell them they didn't stand a chance. I loved her like the sister I'd always wanted. Sadie was dressed in a hot pink Lilly Pulitzer shift dress with a floral print. Very few people could pull that off, but she created a striking picture walking into the coffee shop. Sadie dated, but she had never been serious with anyone. Her life really revolved around me and the girls.

"Hey, Emmy," Sadie said, planting a kiss on my head. She went behind the counter and helped herself to some coffee and a bagel. "You look tired. You need a break."

"You're right, as usual. I'll come and sit with you." I grabbed a cup of coffee and joined Sadie at a booth. Instead of telling me about work as she usually did, she jumped right in with much more interesting news.

"Em, there was this guy that came in to the research room today. Let me tell you, he gave the word hot a whole new meaning. Tall and muscular, black hair, and the bluest eyes I've ever seen. He sure made my morning. Believe it or not, he was nice too. He's from Chicago, and explained he is doing some research on Beckland since he just bought a house here. I told him I would help him." Sadie's eyes twinkled as she spoke. "Maybe I'll end up with his phone number and a date before it's over."

"Was his name Liam?" I asked, trying to sound nonchalant. I knew it had to be the same man I had been so mean to earlier. This was a small town, and a new, hot guy was not something that happened every day.

"Um, yes, and you know this how?"

"He came into the coffee shop this morning and introduced himself. He was doing some sort of work at the booth over there. I was really rude to him."

"Why were you impolite? You're the sweetest person I know."

"Well, I was nasty to him. I'm not really sure why. Something about him set me on edge. I can't really explain it," I confessed. "I definitely owe him an apology if I ever see him again. I don't know what came over me."

Sadie and I talked for the remainder of our lunch break. Before she left, we made plans to have a girls' night soon. We hugged goodbye and she headed back to work, and I returned to the back room to finish my inventory. The rest of the afternoon flew by. Before I knew it, it was time to head home to get the girls off the bus. I placed the "Closed" sign on the front door of Morning Glory and locked up.

I walked into my house just as the bus pulled up in front. Lily, Dahlia, and Rose came through the front door. Backpacks and jackets were dropped in the middle of the floor just as they always were. Hugs and kisses were passed around, and each girl started telling me about her day at the same time. It was the beautiful chaos that I loved most about being a mom.

I headed into the kitchen to start dinner. The girls planted themselves around the large kitchen table to do their homework. I jumped in and answered questions, helped Lily study for a geography test, and went over Dahlia's spelling words. Then I read about Rose's class project which was due in two weeks. I sighed, wishing I had more hours in my day.

Two hours later, we sat down to a dinner of spaghetti and meatballs. I was beat. All I could think of was a hot shower and my bed. Unfortunately, I still had the kitchen to clean up, lunches to pack for tomorrow, two loads of laundry to wash and fold, and kids to get ready for bed.

It was eleven o'clock when I finally collapsed. It felt so good to be still. I was going non-stop since six a.m. My days were exhausting. So many things had to be done. Doing them all alone was harder than I ever imagined it would be. In moments like this, I wished I had someone to share the load.

The nights were the worst. I always managed to keep busy during the day so it was easy to push my loneliness aside. When the girls were all asleep and the house was quiet, solitude crept in.

This wasn't the way I imagined my life. I never set out to be a single mom. Jacob and I were supposed to be doing this together. We hadn't always seen eye to eye, and yes, the spark had been gone between us for a long time. I wondered if it had ever been there. Sometimes I was certain that it never existed at all. The one thing we had in common, though, was the girls. That was what kept us together, when we both knew we would have been happier without each other. The sad fact was that our entire marriage was nothing but an obligation for both of us.

I tried not to dwell on my past, and most of the time I was successful. I didn't regret my marriage to Jacob because my daughters were a result of it, and I couldn't ever be sorry for that. I had been so disillusioned by the whole mess of it that I vowed never to become involved with another man again. I would rather be lonely.

Most of the time I was fine with this decision, but there were times when I missed that feeling of partnership. Sometimes at night, the isolation nearly consumed me. I slept with the television on just for the sounds. I hated the quiet. All of my fears and thoughts of failure bred within silence.

It wasn't as if I had to be alone. I'd had plenty of

offers of dates and more since Jacob's death. I wasn't interested. There was a part of me that died inside on the day his infidelity was confirmed. I had lost my trusting nature, and now assumed the worst when it came to men. As I thought of Jacob's betrayal, I felt a fresh surge of anger. I couldn't believe how much it still hurt, even after all this time. What he had done was unforgivable. I was determined never to be that vulnerable again. Exhaustion took over my thoughts. My eyelids grew heavy. Strangely, the last thought I had before drifting off to sleep was Liam and his sea- blue eyes.

Chapter Three

The next morning was hectic again. Chaotic mornings seemed to be my new normal. I headed over to Morning Glory after the girls left for school. I jumped right in to work, knowing I needed to finish my inventory accounting. My preference would have been to avoid this task like the plague, but instead, I opted to finish it as quickly as possible. I am not a natural businesswoman, and money matters hold little interest to me. It goes with the territory, though, and I knew I had to get it done. However, before long, Sadie arrived for lunch. Once we were settled into our usual table, she began talking.

"So, I spent the morning helping that guy, Liam, we were talking about yesterday." I noticed she had a definite twinkle in her eye again when she mentioned him. "Let me just say that most men can only dream of being that degree of beautiful."

I rolled my eyes as Sadie went on and on about Liam. She talked about men all the time. Usually I found it entertaining, because I lived vicariously through my best friend's love life. Hearing her talk about Liam irritated me, though. I don't know why, but I didn't like hearing that she and Liam had hit if off so well. Then I scolded myself for my reaction. Of course, he was interested in her. All men were interested in Sadie. I would have questioned his vision if he hadn't been. It shouldn't bother me that they had spent the morning together. The man was a complete stranger to me, not to mention, I had been anything but kind to him the day before. He certainly wasn't interested in me.

"Liam supposedly bought a house in town. I think he's a cop or something. He's staying at a hotel until his furniture arrives. I don't know where the house is. He's been kind of vague about the research. He just asks questions about the town and I answer him. He seems mysterious," Sadie finished, interrupting my wayward thoughts.

"Well, if anyone can help him, it's you, Sadie," I said, pushing my jealousy aside. "No one knows the history of Beckland like you do."

"Thank you, my dear." She smiled. "Well, I'm back to work. Are we still on for pizza and bowling with the kiddos tonight?"

"Yes, I couldn't get out of it even if I tried." I laughed, thinking of how excited the girls were to see Sadie. "Come down around six this evening and we'll drive over together."

***

Sadie waltzed through the door right on time. She was nothing, if not prompt. Of course, it didn't take her long to walk from her apartment upstairs. She looked like sheer perfection, as usual. I swear, the woman could have stepped out of a magazine. In contrast, I was a hot mess. I was tired and sweaty from running around doing my afternoon chores. I hadn't even bothered to change out of my work clothes. What I really wanted was a nap. She arrived just as I was trying to persuade the girls to put their shoes on.

"Aunt Sadie!" screamed the three girls in unison, as they jumped into her open arms.

I watched as my girls and my best friend embraced. Sadie was truly a part of our little family. It didn't matter if we were not blood relatives. I was grateful every day for her.

Our little group headed outside, got into my blue SUV, and drove across town to Sam's Bowling. Sam's had been a part of Beckland for as long as I could remember. I had spent many Friday nights here as a teenager, bowling with my friends. The place smelled like pizza, beer, and bowling shoes, but I loved it. It was full of memories.

We chose our lane, put on our bowling shoes, and placed our pizza order. We were fully immersed in our game when I looked across the room and saw him. My heart skipped a beat, and I involuntarily caught my breath. I could feel the heat rise in my body, and I felt my face flush. I hadn't covered my reaction well, and my gasp was loud enough for Sadie to notice. Following my stare, she spotted Liam walking through the front door. I know for a fact that Sadie had never seen me react this way toward a man before, mostly because I never had. I certainly hadn't reacted this way to Jacob.

"You okay, Em?"

"Um, yeah, sure, I think it's your turn." I hoped she wouldn't comment on my reaction to Liam's arrival. I prayed to myself that he wouldn't spot us and come over. Apparently, heaven was not on my side tonight, because he saw us and headed straight toward our lane.

"Sadie, hello, I thought that was you." Liam gave Sadie a quick hug. "Thanks so much for your help today. I really feel like I learned something about Beckland. I figure since I'm going to be living here, I should know more about the town."

Sadie and Liam conversed easily for a couple of minutes. I mentally kicked myself as that twinge of jealousy again reared its ugly head. Sadie was stunning and charming, and Liam was obviously interested. I looked down at my old jeans and ratty shirt and made a mental note that maybe I should take a bit more time with my appearance. Not that it mattered. Sadie and Liam obviously had hit it off quite well. They looked like old friends.

And why should I care, anyway? I certainly didn't have any claims on the man. I wasn't even interested in men. Besides, I was fully aware I couldn't compete with my best friend in the looks department. There weren't many men who would ever choose me over Sadie. I was having a difficult time coming to terms with my reaction to him, though. It was becoming hard to ignore.

"It's Emma, right?" asked Liam, turning away from

Sadie, and offering me his outstretched hand. "We met in your coffee shop."

"Good memory. Yes, it's Emma," I reluctantly shook Liam's hand.

As our hands clasped, I couldn't describe it, but something happened. It felt like a bolt of lightning shot straight out of Liam and arced into me. I had never felt anything like that before in my life. Like an idiot, I actually jumped and dropped his hand like it was a hot coal. Surprise was written all over his face, while mine turned an even brighter shade of red, partly from embarrassment, and partly from the heat that was radiating inside of me.

What was it about this man? When Liam looked at me, I felt naked. I felt like he was looking right into my soul. It was certainly disturbing. I didn't like the vulnerable feeling that I had around him. I knew without a doubt that he had felt that jolt as well. Not knowing what to do, I turned away.

Sadie stood back, watching the scene unfold right in front of her. She had known me her whole life. She knew my every quirk. She could practically read my mind. She could tell immediately sparks flew between us. The chemistry was tangible. Sadie looked at me as if she might say something, but, thankfully, kept her mouth shut. I wished she would somehow rescue me before I made an even bigger idiot of myself.

I was so flustered by the encounter with Liam I didn't know what to do. I couldn't bring myself to look at him. How could a handshake be so intimate? I searched for something to distract me. Grabbing my purse, I searched for something, anything to occupy my hands. About that time, my daughters noticed there was a new face in our little group.

"Aunt Sadie, who's he?" asked Dahlia, pointing toward Liam.

"Yeah, Aunt Sadie, is this another new boyfriend?"

Rose giggled.

Lily just stood off to the side watching.

"No, this isn't my boyfriend. His name is Liam O'Reilly and he's new in town and doing some research. I've been helping him over at the library. I think he knows your mom, too, from the looks of things," Sadie added with a grin.

"He doesn't know our mom. If he knew our mom, we would know him," said Lily defensively.

"You're right, Lily, I actually don't know your mom very well. I only met her yesterday. I was in her coffee shop, and I introduced myself," Liam explained quickly, perceptive enough to notice that Lily was protective of me. "It's nice to meet you girls."

Rose and Dahlia politely shook hands, but Lily simply nodded her regal little head.

I didn't know what to say. I sat on the bench, completely mute through the entire exchange. Liam threw me off balance. The only way I knew to deal with him was to avoid him. He didn't make that easy, though, with his open personality and beautiful eyes. And why was I so obsessed with the man's eyes, anyway?

I tried my best to get through the rest of the game. When the pizza arrived, I didn't eat any. I wasn't sure how I was supposed to swallow pizza over the lump in my throat, not to mention I was so flustered by his proximity that I began to feel nauseous. Thankfully, the game ended and the pizza was gone, and it was time to go home. I couldn't get out of there quickly enough. Sadie and Liam stood chatting easily with each other. I felt my irritation grow again watching the two of them together.

"Sadie, we need to go. The girls are tired and so am I," I said tersely.

"Yeah, sure, Em," Sadie was suddenly aware of my agitation. "Liam, I will probably see you at the library tomorrow." Sadie and the girls went to the door ahead of me, leaving me alone with Liam.

"Emma, it was a pleasure talking with you again. Your daughters are beautiful, but that's no surprise with you as their mother." Liam stopped me in my tracks. He was certainly a smooth operator, and probably knew just what to say to women to make them turn to mush. Well, not me!

"Goodbye Liam," I said rudely as I walked quickly past him and headed outside. I was sure Liam was puzzled by my abruptness, but I didn't care. I needed to stay far away from that man for my own good. He was dangerous.

Out in the parking lot, I loaded the girls into the SUV without a word. Sadie watched me with a confused look on her face, probably trying to figure out why I was so crazy. I was suddenly embarrassed at how unkind I had been to Liam. I didn't normally treat people that way. I could feel Sadie's knowing gaze upon me. At that moment, I wished she didn't know me so well.

Sadie had no doubt noticed the fiery chemistry between me and Liam, too. I'm sure she wasn't going to let this rest. What was that? Although I didn't date, I had encountered men that I was attracted to. In all my life, I had never experienced the chemistry I felt from that simple handshake. This was way out of my comfort zone. We rode home in silence. The girls were worn out from the busy day. I couldn't wait to get them into bed. I needed some time to figure out what was going on inside of my head. Sadie came in and helped me get the girls into their pajamas. They brushed their teeth, and we tucked them in. When we were alone in my kitchen, Sadie unleashed on me.

"Em, what was that about at the bowling alley? You were so mean to Liam." Sadie went straight to the point. "I have never seen you act like that, and don't even try and tell me that you aren't attracted to him. I'm surprised the bowling alley didn't spontaneously combust from all of the sparks you two were giving off."

"I don't know what you're talking about," I replied defiantly. "I am not interested in that man in the very least."

I walked over to the sink and put water into the teapot. I could feel Sadie's eyes on me, watching the rigid way I was holding myself. I was a ball of stress. I couldn't hide from her. "Em, I know you better than anyone. What I saw back there with the two of you, no way can you say that you didn't feel it. It was obvious to me and anyone else who was watching. There is a serious spark there. Why don't you just admit it?"

"Okay, fine," I said, exasperated that I was so transparent. "I admit it. There's something about him that I'm drawn to. I'm attracted to him, and that scares me. I don't have the time or the temperament for men."

"Look, hon, I know Jacob hurt you. The man was a lying jerk. I never did like him. But sooner or later, you have got to move past that. You don't want to end up alone." Sadie wrapped me into her arms.

"I'm not alone. I have the girls, and I have you. I don't need anything else," I replied stubbornly, sounding like Rose when she was pouting.

"Of course you have us. But one of these days, your girls are going to grow up and have their own lives. As for me, I sure hope I'm not going to be single forever. I love you, Em, but don't let Jacob steal anything else from you. He's not worth it."

"You don't know how hard it is for me. I don't trust anyone. I don't think I ever will. I'm hopeless, Sadie," I said desperately.

"You're not hopeless, you're just tired. I'm going home now. Go get a warm shower and go to bed. You look awful," Sadie teased.

"Thanks a lot." I laughed. "See you tomorrow."

I locked the door behind Sadie and headed upstairs

to my room. Carrying my pajamas into the bathroom, I turned on the hot water in the shower, and let it wash over me. It didn't wash away the knot inside of my stomach, though. I knew that I had to let go of the hurt and betrayal of Jacob, but I didn't know how. I had been angry at him for so many years.

In some ways, the anger helped me mask the hurt. As long as I was angry, I didn't have to feel the pain. I didn't have time for all of this. I didn't have time for love, and relationships, and Liam and his stupid blue eyes. I wished he would just go back to where he came from and let me get back to normal. My life certainly wasn't exciting, but it was predictable, and I knew how to handle that. Liam struck me as being anything but predictable.

Chapter Four

I stood laughing and chatting with a couple of my regular customers the next morning. I decided to forget about Liam. I definitely didn't want to get involved. As long as I avoided him, I wouldn't have to deal with the feelings that were developing for the man. I heard the bell on the front door jingle, announcing a customer. I looked up from my conversation. My heart flip-flopped when he walked through the door. His constant presence was making it extremely difficult to forget about him. He definitely caused a reaction in me that I was having a hard time ignoring. He flashed a dazzling smile, and headed straight toward me. My palms began to sweat, and I wiped them on my pants.

"Good morning, Emma. You're looking lovely today. I'd like a coffee, if you're not too busy."

"Of course, I'll bring it over to you." I forced myself to answer him politely.

I poured his coffee with trembling hands. At this rate, I would end up spilling it all over him. Taking a calming breath, I headed to Liam's table.

"Here you are," I said, sitting the coffee on the table, trying not to make direct eye contact.

"Emma, I'm not sure how I've offended you, but I get the feeling you are trying to avoid me." Liam said, causing me to look at him. His kind face was smiling back at me. I felt my guard go down a little.

"You haven't offended me at all. I don't know what has been wrong with me lately, just tired I guess," I answered reluctantly, feeling the need to explain away my bad behavior.

"Well, that's no wonder. I'm sure it's exhausting keeping up with all you have to do. Maybe you can take a break and join me for some coffee?"

"I'll have to ask the boss." I smiled at him for the

first time.

I decided I could at least be civil to Liam. After all, he was new in town, and he was nice. He had never done anything to deserve my animosity. It was not his fault that I was completely insane and couldn't trust myself around him. I tried to rationalize that we could just be friends. Who was I kidding, though? The feelings I was having toward him were more than just friendly. I stood there waging a war inside of my mind while Liam looked at me expectantly. Reluctantly, I slid into the booth opposite him. Once I took a breath and convinced myself to pretend to be normal, we chatted easily for the next fifteen minutes.

"Thanks for the break, Liam. I need to get back to work, though," I said kindly. "It really was nice getting to know you."

"You too, Emma. I'm sure we will bump into each other again soon."

Liam gathered his belongings and headed out the front door.

I watched him go, thinking how nice it had been talking to him. He was easygoing and seemed genuinely kind. He wasn't at all what I thought he would be like. I warned myself that I couldn't make it a habit, though, or that would be dangerous for my heart.

***

Walking out the front door of the coffee shop, Liam felt a twinge of anxiety. Things were not going as planned. He was here to do a job, not flirt with the widow of the man he was investigating. He needed to stick to the itinerary. His job was to find out where Jacob and Veronica had stashed the jewels, plain and simple. Emma was nothing more than a means to an end. Yes, he needed to befriend her. He needed to make her trust him so that she spoke freely about her late husband. What he didn't need was to fall for her. There was something about her, though. Each time he saw her, he found himself wanting to know her better. He enjoyed her company, and kept inventing new ways to be near her. Liam reminded himself that the job had to come first. No matter how attracted he was to Emma, he would not allow himself to fall for her. Taking one last look into the coffee shop window at her, he quickly walked away.

Chapter Five

After the girls got home from school the following Monday afternoon, a unanimous decision was made that it was far too beautiful to spend indoors. We headed down the street to the park. I sat on the bench watching the girls play ball. It was a gorgeous spring day, and there wasn't a cloud in the sky.

Beckland in the spring, in my opinion, personified the perfect small town. It was quaint and idyllic, and an absolute safe haven. Most people didn't even lock their doors. Unlike the city, it felt welcoming, and I was happy to be raising my girls here. I knew everyone and everyone knew me. There was a feeling of security here that couldn't be found in larger cities.

The trees were starting to bloom, there were flowers popping up everywhere, and a lingering freshness was in the air. Dahlia and Rose were kicking a soccer ball back and forth, laughing and running. Lily was even joining in the game. It was so good to watch them playing, carefree as children should be.

I glanced around, watching a dad push his daughter on the swings. A part of me was always a little sad when I saw other children with their fathers. My father had been amazing, and I couldn't imagine how my childhood would have been without him. It made me realize just what my girls were missing out on.

I thought back on the time my dad had taken me fishing. He wanted me to like it so much. I couldn't get over the slimy worms and the smell of fish. I hadn't enjoyed it as much as he had hoped, but I remembered how nice it was just hanging out with him. I got lost in the daydream, forgetting myself for a few minutes.

I was suddenly torn from my reverie when I heard Dahlia scream. I jumped up, dread filling me, thoughts of broken arms or legs, or one of them being kidnapped.

Looking for the girls, I located them just in time to see the ball rolling into the street and Rose running after it. My heart stopped. How many times had I told her not to run into the street without looking? She was oblivious of the car headed straight for her. She was too far away from me, and I knew I couldn't get to her in time. Panic-stricken, I did the only thing I could. I screamed loudly for Rose to stop, but my daughter was on a mission.

Fear gave way to adrenaline, and I ran as fast as I could toward her, knowing I would never get there in time. I was living every parent's worst nightmare.

Finally, Rose heard me screaming, and looked up as the car was within inches of her. Her face registered panic, but instead of moving, she froze in place. From out of nowhere, a large man placed his body between Rose and the car, grabbed her, and moved her to safety. The car skidded to a screeching halt just in the nick of time. Running for all I was worth, I reached Rose as she and the man collapsed onto the sidewalk. My heart raced and I was gulping air, trying to catch my breath.

I snatched Rose from the arms of her rescuer, suddenly realizing it was Liam. Where had he come from? He had saved my daughter's life. I knew without a doubt if he hadn't been there at that exact second, the car would have hit her.

I held on tightly to Rose, like a drowning person clinging to a life raft. I remember thinking I was never going to let my little girl out of my arms again. I had almost lost her. I fell to pieces, sobbing and cradling her in my arms there on the sidewalk. I was crying, and Rose was crying. Dahlia and Lily, who had run over to us, were both crying too. If Liam hadn't been at the right place at the right time, I knew this would have ended very differently.

"Liam, I don't even know what to say. You saved my baby's life." I stood, looking at him. I think I was in shock, and I started trembling uncontrollably. "I don't have words right now."

"Is she okay? I was trying not to crush her when I grabbed her. Did I hurt her?"

"Hurt her? Liam, she would have been hit by that car if it weren't for you." I was stricken anew with the knowledge of how close the vehicle had come to hitting Rose.

At that moment, my tears started again. I was generally not the weepy type, but the thought of losing my baby was enough to send me over the edge. I collapsed onto the sidewalk, cradling all three of my girls in my arms. The thought of losing one of my children was incomprehensible.

Liam stood, probably knowing someone needed to take control of the situation. I was certainly in no condition to make sound decisions. He told me that we were going back to my house to take a closer look at Rose and make sure she was okay. He leaned down and took Rose from me, carrying her in his arms toward the house. Lily, Dahlia, and I followed, glad that he had taken the reins.

When we arrived home, we sat Rose on the couch in the living room. Rose hadn't said a word.

"Rose, honey, are you okay? Does anything hurt?" I prompted.

"No, mama," Rose said quietly, her head hanging. All at once, the tears started. They soon turned into sobs. "I'm sorry, mama. I know I shouldn't have run into the street. You always tell me to pay attention, and I didn't. I just wanted to get the ball."

"Rose, sweetie, I'm not mad at you. I was just so scared. Please don't do that to me, ever again!"

"Thank you for saving me," Rose said shyly to Liam, wiping her tears with her small hands.

"Honey, I am so glad I was there and got to you in time," Liam answered with a smile.

"Girls, why don't you go and have some quiet time

in your rooms, please. It's been an exhausting afternoon, and you still have some homework to finish up tonight."

Obediently, the three girls headed upstairs to their rooms. They were obviously exhausted, as they never did homework without an argument.

"Liam, would you like some tea?" I asked awkwardly, suddenly realizing the man I was attracted to was in my home. So much for keeping my distance.

"I would love some, actually." He followed me into the kitchen.

I went to the sink and put some water into the teapot. I placed it on the burner and turned it on; glad I had that small task to keep my hands occupied. Now that Liam and I were alone, I felt nervous. What was I thinking, asking him to stay for tea? I should have politely thanked him and sent him on his way. Way to go, Emma.

But he had saved my daughter's life. The thought kept racing through my head. I had treated him badly nearly every single time I had spoken to him. Guilt gnawed at me. I knew I had to apologize for my unfriendliness.

"Um, Liam, I really need to say something to you," I began, trying to find the right words. "I want to apologize for the way I've acted toward you. I promise I'm really a nice person. I don't know why, but every time you're close to me, my guard goes up, and I end up being rude. You seem to bring out the worst in me."

"Yeah, I noticed that," he said with a laugh. "How about we start over?"

"I'd like that." I was relieved he was so agreeable. He had given me an easy out.

Liam walked toward me, and my palms began to sweat. What was he doing? Why wasn't he sitting down anymore? I was sure my heart was going to explode inside of my chest. I was about to have a heart attack and he was going to have to call the paramedics for me. I would die of embarrassment.

He stood in front of me, a mere couple of inches away. I tipped my head up to see his face. Those blue eyes looked down at me, and I was lost. Any thoughts I might have had about keeping my distance were immediately swept away when he looked at me. Slowly, Liam bent down and cupped my face in his hands, gently caressing my cheek with his thumb. He just stood there and looked at me. Time stood still. I probably looked like an idiot. I could do nothing, but stare back at him, lost in the moment. I thought he was going to kiss me, but he didn't. He just kept looking at me, as if he were seeing into my very soul.

The moment was interrupted by the whistling of the teapot. It startled me so much that I jumped. Laughing nervously, I broke away and headed to the stove. Turning off the burner, I made the tea, my head spinning. What was I doing? What had just happened? Liam and I had most definitely just had a "moment." I was quickly losing the battle with myself to stay strong and keep my distance, but maybe I didn't really want to fight it anymore.

I placed Liam's tea in front of him, along with sugar and cream.

"Thank you, Emma. So now what?"

"Now what? I'm not sure what you mean," I lied.

"Come on, Emma. Let's stop playing games. There is something between us, you know it, and I know it. There's no reason to try and deny it anymore."

Darn that man! He was so open and kind, my defenses didn't stand a chance. What should I say? Should I continue to pretend I didn't know what he was talking about? Or should I listen to my heart for the first time in years, and see where it led me?

"Fine, I'm not going to deny it." I was being honest for the first time in a long time. " I felt something the moment I saw you. I can't explain it, but it was definitely there. I've been trying to ignore it and hide from it, but I keep coming back to it. That's the reason I've been so rude.

I feel like I need to keep my distance, but I can't seem to. I don't know what to do from here. It's been a long time since I've felt this way. Maybe I've never felt this way."

"Yeah, I actually understand that. It sounds pretty similar to the way I've been feeling." Liam laughed. "I don't know what to do either. Maybe we should start by going on a date? Dinner, something, I don't know."

"Go on a date? I feel strangely like I'm back in high school all of a sudden," I giggled. "Yes, a date. I would like that very much, I think. Where would we go?"

"I know this great little coffee shop..." Liam laughed. "Seriously, though, I would like to take you somewhere really nice. What do you think about that Italian place on Russell Street?"

"Vinnie's? That place is pretty fancy," I said, not used to dressing up and going to fancy places.

"You deserve to be treated well. I will pick you up tomorrow night at seven."

"Okay, but what about the girls? I need to ask Sadie if she can sit with them. A date? Wow, maybe I shouldn't..." I stammered at the realization of what I had just agreed to. My pulse was racing, and I was trying to figure out how I could backtrack and change my answer.

"Emma, I will see you tomorrow at seven. I'm sure Sadie will be happy to watch the girls. Be ready," Liam said, bending down and touching his lips lightly to mine. It caught me so off guard that I could do nothing but nod, as Liam walked out the front door.

I grabbed the counter. I was reeling. I had just agreed to a dinner date with Liam. What was I thinking? I didn't date! Liam had just kissed me. I had to steady myself. Without another thought, I grabbed the phone and called Sadie.

***

Liam walked out of Emma's front door. He wasn't exactly sure what had just happened, but he couldn't seem to wipe the smile off of his face. He certainly hadn't planned on kissing Emma, or asking her out to dinner. He couldn't seem to keep his head in the game when he was in the same room with her. He felt out of control when he was around her, and he wasn't sure if he liked it or not.

His mind was reeling with everything that had transpired over the last hour. He had saved Rose's life. That was a bit much for him to wrap his head around, but he was grateful he had been there. Emma's daughters were so sweet. He thought of Rose's little face as she looked up at him, thanking him for saving her. His heart cracked wide open.

Although he knew he shouldn't be getting involved, he couldn't resist the beautiful, vulnerable Emma. It wasn't part of the plan. Liam was very much a "stick to the facts" kind of guy. His job trained him never to get personally involved in a case. For all his training, though, nothing could have prepared him for the intense feelings he was having for Emma. He always hoped he would find the right woman one day. Until now, playing by the rules had worked for him. Maybe it was time for once to make them up as he went. Tomorrow night could not get here fast enough.

Chapter Six

For the first time in weeks, I woke up before the alarm went off. My first thought upon opening my eyes was that I had a date tonight. I was going on a date with Liam. It was such a foreign idea that I had to repeat it to myself a couple of times. My stomach was tied up in knots. I hadn't been on a date since high school! What was I going to wear?

I decided I had to get through the first part of my day before I could focus on the second. I headed upstairs to wake the girls and begin the craziness. I sailed through the rest of the morning and afternoon in a fog. I had a hard time focusing on work. My thoughts kept going back to Liam and yesterday in my kitchen. I felt lightheaded just thinking about being close to him, and the kiss had been spectacular. It all happened so quickly that I hadn't had time to process it. I knew one thing for sure; I was doing a terrible job of keeping my distance.

Finally, work was finished and I headed home. Sadie had excitedly agreed to watch the girls, and was even picking them up from school and taking them out for pizza. She was overjoyed that I was going on a date after all these years. To top it off, they were spending the night upstairs with her, so I didn't have anything to focus on except myself, which was a rare occurrence for me.

The house was empty when I went inside. I had three hours to myself. I couldn't remember the last time I had been alone in my own home. I decided I was going to pamper myself. I grabbed the romance novel I had been meaning to start, and headed upstairs to my bathroom. I opened the cupboard door, looked way in the back, and grabbed the vanilla scented bubble bath I hadn't used in forever. Turning on the water in my claw-foot bathtub, I generously dumped in the bubble bath. Undressing, I stepped into the steamy water, lowering my body beneath the bubbles. I sighed with contentment, as I eased myself down even lower. Relaxing moments were few and far between in my world. It had been months since I had taken the time to luxuriate in a bubble bath. I filled the tub until it was up to my chin. I grabbed my novel and began reading.

Forty-five minutes later, I realized the water was no longer hot. I quickly washed my hair, shaved my legs, and grabbed my towel. Drying off, I caught a glimpse of myself in the mirror. For the first time in a long time, I took a good, long look. I very rarely gave my naked body any thought, but I looked closely at it now. My fair skin had a rosy glow to it, thanks to the hot bath. I was not tall, and not short. I didn't have the long legs that I admired on other women. I was curvier than most, but thought I carried it well. I had an ample chest, rounded hips, and a few stretch marks from my pregnancies. I didn't think I looked too bad for a thirty-year-old woman. I wasn't a runway model, but I had always been satisfied with my appearance. Inspecting myself in the mirror, I began to feel a bit self-conscious thinking of Liam seeing me naked. I was startled at my own thought process. Where had that come from?

"Well, be reasonable, Emma," I said to myself. "You're both grown adults. You are obviously attracted to each other. It's the logical progression, right?"

If I had been nervous before, I was even more so now. Thinking of where this night might lead put a whole new spin on the nervousness. I scolded myself, certain I was jumping the gun by thinking that Liam and I would hit it off so well that we ended the night in bed. That was nonsense. I wasn't even the kind of woman to do such a thing. I wasn't so easily won over. I stood there forcing myself to take deep, calming breaths, and decided I needed to get myself ready for my date. Otherwise, Liam was going to show up and I would still be standing there staring at my naked self in the mirror.

I took extra care with my makeup, applying a bit

more than usual. I grabbed my hair dryer, deciding I was going to put some extra effort into my hair tonight. I styled my long, wavy, strawberry blonde hair with care, admiring the result when I was done. I stepped back and looked at my reflection in the mirror.

"Not too bad, Em."

Going into my closet, I took the green dress from the back. It had been four years since I had last worn it, and I was hoping it still fit. I had splurged on the beautiful dress for a fancy girls' dinner that Sadie had conned me into. She had taken me out in hopes of finding me a man. I quickly crushed her dreams. I had only worn it that one night, and it had hung in my closet ever since.

I spritzed my body with vanilla perfume, generously applied some body lotion, and grabbed my nicest bra and panty set. I pulled the emerald green dress over my frame, and sighed with relief when it still fit perfectly.

Standing in front of the full-length mirror, I looked at the finished product. I was startled at the woman who looked back at me. It was quite a transformation. It was me, only better. My hair was perfect, my makeup was expertly applied, and I knew the emerald dress brought out the color of my eyes.

My thoughts were interrupted by the doorbell ringing. I began having a minor panic attack. I was suddenly second guessing my decision to go out with Liam. I couldn't go on a date! I had sworn off of men. I certainly couldn't let myself get mixed up with this man, who set my heart on fire by his mere existence!

"Snap out of it, Em," I scolded myself. "Don't be an idiot. Answer the door."

Taking a deep breath, I headed down the stairs, nervously opening the front door. If I thought, Liam looked good before, that was nothing compared to how he looked tonight. He had on a gray suit, perfectly tailored to his exquisite body. His black hair was still wet, and playfully curled around his ears. His sea-blue eyes locked onto me and time stood still. I was riveted in place, drinking in the sight of him, while he did the same with me.

"Emma, you are stunning," Liam said quietly, fixing his gaze on me.

"Right back at ya," I said shyly. I mentally kicked myself for not having a more appropriate response.

Liam took my hand in his, and led me down the front steps to his car, a shiny black Mustang. Of course, a man like Liam would drive a black Mustang. What else would he drive? Could he be more attractive to me right now? He opened the car door, and helped me in before he walked around to the driver's side. We drove across town in companionable silence, arriving a few minutes later at Vinnie's.

Liam jumped out of the car and came around to open my door and help me out. He took my hand and he didn't let go. We walked into the restaurant, linked to each other. We were immediately seated at a window table. The white tablecloths and candlelight created the perfect setting. This restaurant was built for romance. Liam pulled my chair out and waited for me to be seated before he walked over to his own chair and sat. We looked at each other for a couple of minutes, words seemingly unnecessary. I didn't think I would ever get tired of looking at him. My heart beat nervously.

"Emma, I know I said it before, but you are truly beautiful. You stole my breath away when you opened the front door." He smiled.

"Thank you Liam. I almost didn't answer, I was so nervous."

"Well, I am sure glad that you did." He reached across the table for my hand. It seemed perfectly natural to put it into his.

We ordered our meals, and easily chatted with each other while we waited for our food to arrive. I was surprised at how easily the conversation flowed. The nervousness I had felt earlier was completely gone.

"So, tell me about your life, Liam. I feel like we have gone about this all backward. We are so close already, but I know nothing about you, really."

"Well, there's not a lot to tell. I'm an FBI agent, which sounds way more exciting than it actually is. I'm originally from Chicago. My parents emigrated from Ireland, so I'm a first-generation American. I regret to say that I have inherited the Irish temper, but have learned to control it. I just bought the house in Beckland, so I guess I'm from here now. I haven't ever been married, and I don't have any kids, much to my parents' dismay. I honestly haven't even dated much, because work has always gotten in the way. I've been pretty focused on my career up to now, mostly because no one has gotten my attention enough to distract me...until a few days ago, that is. I have definitely found myself distracted by you. I would love to hear more about you."

"Wow, about me...okay. My life certainly doesn't compare with the adventure you're used to. Instead of chasing criminals around all day, I run after my kids. Being a mom and running a coffee shop is not that exciting. And unfortunately, there's really nothing more to tell." I was fully aware how boring my life must sound to someone like Liam.

"That's not true. You definitely excite me." A spark of mischief danced in his cerulean eyes. "I also know there's more to you than work and kids. Tell me about when you were younger. What did you want to do? How did you meet your husband?"

"Jacob and I knew each other our whole lives. We were both born and raised in Beckland, and went to school together from the time we were kids. Jacob decided I was "his" when we were in high school. He was handsome and popular, and no one said no to him. I guess I just went along with it when he decided we were an item. I was pretty shy, and considered myself lucky to be noticed by him. It sounds really stupid, doesn't it? I never questioned it. We dated all through high school, he proposed, and I said yes. All I really wanted to do was have kids, and it seemed like the logical thing to do. I thought I loved him, but I know now that I had no idea what that really meant," I stopped, suddenly self-conscious that I had revealed too much. I didn't want to bore Liam with the details of my mundane life.

"Go on, Emma. Tell me more. Were you and Jacob happy?"

"I wouldn't say we were happy, exactly, but we weren't miserable. Does that even make any sense? I immediately got pregnant with Lily, then Dahlia, then Rose. It all happened so fast, and I was happy to be a mom. I had everything I dreamed of in my girls, but things with Jacob were pretty stagnant. I knew we shouldn't have gotten married. I figured that out pretty quickly, but I had made a commitment to him and to my kids, so I was determined to stick it out. Sounds pretty heroic, doesn't it? I realize now, I was just afraid to make a change,"

"I think it actually does sound heroic, Emma. There aren't enough couples who stay true to the commitment they make to be a family."

"Well, the problem was that only one of us stayed true to that commitment. I found out when Jacob died that he had been having an affair with our neighbor, Veronica, for quite some time. Apparently, I was too stupid to see it. Or maybe I did see it, but didn't want to admit it. Looking back, there were clues all over the place. I let myself be blind to them. I didn't want to see them, because I was afraid of what I would have to do if I did. Anyway, in some ways I was set free when Jacob died, as horrible as that sounds. I am nothing, if not blindly loyal, so I would have stayed with him forever, even though I was unsatisfied."

I took a breath and sat back, startled at how much I had revealed to Liam. I couldn't believe how easy it was to talk to him. There was nothing forced or awkward about it. I honestly thought I could tell him anything and he would listen and not judge. That was a rare quality in a person. I was beginning to realize there was much more to Liam than just a handsome face.

"Wow, I just sort of vomited out my life at you, didn't I?" I laughed as I felt the tension slip out of my body.

"I'm glad you did. I'm glad you feel comfortable with me, Emma. I can't even put into words how I'm feeling. It's like we've known each other for years, not just a few days. Usually I'm pretty guarded with people, especially women. I've seen a lot with my job, and it's made me cynical, I guess. With you, though, I'm at home. Does that sound ridiculous?"

"It doesn't sound ridiculous at all, Liam. I feel the exact same way, and Lord knows I've tried my best not to." I was grateful that I wasn't the only one entering unchartered territory. It seemed like the world had been put into fast forward mode, and Liam and I had known each other for years, not just a few days. How was it possible to experience this level of intimacy with someone after such a short time? It usually took me years to let my guard down with people.

We continued our easy conversation through the rest of dinner. We shared tiramisu for dessert, and had another glass of wine to top it off. The easiness with Liam was unexpected. We decided to go for a walk after dinner. It was such a beautiful night, and neither of us was ready for it to end. We strolled hand in hand. It was perfect.

On the drive back to my house, the nervousness began. It had been a long time since I was in this position, and I wasn't really sure how to proceed. Should I invite Liam in? Was that too presumptuous? Was that even an expectation? I did have the house to myself, which I was sure Sadie had thought of when she offered to have the girls sleep at her place. But did I want to put myself in the position of being alone with Liam, knowing where that could lead? A million questions raced through my head until I felt like it was going to explode. As usual, I was overanalyzing the situation. Finally, I just decided not to overthink it, and go with my gut. It was new for me, but I was quickly realizing I didn't have all of the answers anymore. I was operating on pure instinct at this point, and maybe that was okay.

We arrived at my house, and Liam opened the car door and helped me out. We walked to the porch, where he paused by the front door. I could tell he was as unsure as I was about how to proceed.

"Emma, I don't want to assume that you want me to come inside, but in case you were thinking of asking, the answer would be yes." Liam looked straight into my eyes.

Instead of answering, I leaned toward him, pulled his face down to mine, and brushed my lips against his. It started out as a gentle kiss, but quickly turned to something else. Something inside of me awakened with the kiss, and I knew it was too late to stop now.

Fumbling in my purse for the house keys, I quickly located them and we went inside. Once inside, all bets were off. Without taking a minute to question my actions, I took his hand, led him upstairs, and down the hallway to my room. I closed my bedroom door. In that instant, nothing outside of my room existed. We were in a world of our own.

Liam walked toward me and engulfed me in his arms. He kissed me with such passion that I was lost. I returned his kiss, wrapping myself around him. Hands exploring, falling on to the bed, we were lost in one another. I had never felt this kind of passion and urgency. I needed him like I needed air to breathe.

Suddenly, I snapped back to reality. The cynical and mistrusting voice in my head emerged and began its warnings. What was I doing? Was I really going to sleep with Liam? Then what? I knew I wasn't ready for this. I had to stop. I pulled back, standing up and pacing across my bedroom floor.

"Liam, I'm sorry, but I don't think I can do this. I can't give myself to you for one night. I thought I could be reckless and spontaneous, but that's just not me. I am the exact opposite of reckless and spontaneous. I'm guarded and careful. I can't do casual sex. I'm way too attracted to you already. If we put sex in the mix, there'll be no turning back for me," I could hear the desperation in my voice. I wasn't sure if I was trying to convince Liam or myself.

"Emma, look at me. Who said anything about one night? Have I led you to believe that this is casual in any way for me?" He approached me and tipped my head up so he could look into my eyes. "The minute I saw you, that was it for me. I'll be here for tonight, and tomorrow night, and for as many nights as you want me."

"I don't know what to say. I feel drawn to you, and at home with you. That really scares me. I don't get scared too often, but I've been terrified since the first time I laid eyes on you. I know I could lose myself to you. Maybe I already have." My heart pounded quickly as I admitted the truth between us.

"Emma, I just want to be close to you. We don't have to do anything you're not ready to do. Tell you what, why don't you go take off that makeup, change into your pajamas, and climb into bed beside me. I promise nothing will happen that you don't want to happen. I will be happy to just hold you all night."

My head was reeling. This guy was too good to be true. I had brought him to my bedroom, kissed him with everything in me, practically ripped his clothes off, and then brought things to a screeching halt as quickly as I started. He deserved to be angry with me, but he wasn't. He just wanted to be close to me. I realized I needed to hang on to this guy.

"You have a deal."

I did as Liam said, and within a few minutes, we were snuggled together in my bed. I couldn't remember the last time I had felt so safe. For the first time in years, I quickly drifted off into a sound sleep, wrapped securely in Liam's arms.

Chapter Seven

I opened my eyes at seven the next morning. It took me a moment to get my bearings and figure out why I was engulfed inside a set of very muscular arms. Moving gently, trying not to awaken the man sleeping next to me, I maneuvered my way out of Liam's embrace. I couldn't believe I had slept with Liam. We had literally *slept*. True to his word, he hadn't pushed me for more. He simply held me all night long, making me feel safe and secure for the first time in ages.

I propped myself up onto my arm and watched him sleep. I marveled at the sight of him, comfortably resting in my bed. He was truly magnificent to look at. He had stripped down to just his boxer shorts to sleep. Looking at his muscular, chiseled body, I wondered how I had resisted doing more than just sleeping. I was momentarily disappointed with my self-control, and was sure it would have been quite an enjoyable experience. But, I knew it was smart to take things slowly. I couldn't afford to make any reckless mistakes that I would regret later.

I decided I would make Liam breakfast in bed. I tiptoed out of the bedroom and downstairs to the kitchen. Looking in the refrigerator, I settled on scrambled eggs, bacon, and toast. I started the coffee brewing, then set to work. I was so engrossed in my meal preparation that I hadn't heard him come into the kitchen. I turned from the stove to wash my hands at the sink, and jumped as I spotted him sitting on the bar stool at the counter.

"How long have you been sitting there?"

"Long enough to know that I enjoy the view." Liam laughed at my obvious discomfort. "Good morning."

"Good morning." I was suddenly shy. "Um, I was thinking we could have some breakfast? I hope you like bacon and eggs."

"They're my favorite. How did you know?" He

gave me his lopsided grin that I'd come to crave.

I stood there a minute, a bit out of my element. I wasn't used to preparing breakfast while a half-naked man sat at my kitchen counter. I swallowed hard, taking in the form of Liam sitting in my kitchen in nothing but his boxer shorts. It was unnerving, and hard for me to concentrate. Luckily, the food was basically finished, so I didn't have to think too hard.

"Well, it's almost done. I hope you're hungry."

I got out two plates and put a generous amount onto Liam's. I poured him a cup of coffee, plated myself some food, and sat at the counter next to him.

"Thanks for breakfast, Emma."

Liam leaned in and cupped my face in his hand, gently kissing me. The room started spinning, and fireworks were going off inside of my body. It was like the Fourth of July in there. My body was trembling, and my insides resembled a bowl of Jell-O. It was a good thing I was sitting down, because I didn't think my legs would have held me up at that point. The man could certainly kiss. I couldn't remember ever being kissed this way in my life. Jacob certainly hadn't produced this reaction. I suddenly was coming to life for the first time. It was scary and exhilarating at the same time.

All too soon, Liam drew his face away from mine. He began hungrily eating the breakfast I had prepared. I was too worked up to eat, so I just picked at my food. I wasn't sure what to say, but wondered if I should apologize for last night. He didn't seem at all upset that I had put a halt to things, but I wanted to be sure.

"Uh, Liam, I'm really sorry about last night. I didn't mean to lead you on, then shift gears on you so fast. I'm just really confused about what I'm feeling, and I'm afraid of messing things up. I'm afraid of getting involved, I'm afraid of trusting someone, I'm afraid of being vulnerable, I'm afraid of my girls getting attached to someone who isn't in it for the long haul. Yeah, you could say I'm just afraid in general. I'm sort of a mess," I finished with a shrug, certain he must think I was crazy.

"Emma, don't apologize. You have nothing to be sorry for. I told you last night, I'm not going anywhere. We can take things as slowly as you need to. I know you've been hurt, but I will do my best to earn your trust. You'll see you can count on me." Liam smiled widely and I noticed the dimple in his left cheek. It was just one of his many endearing traits that I had come to adore.

We finished breakfast while we got to know each other better. I confided in Liam about the loss of my parents, noticing the compassion in his eyes as I spoke. Liam told me about his own parents and how close they were. I learned that he had an older sister, and she had two daughters. He talked about how important his family was to him, and it endeared him to me even more. After that, we both talked about our awkward teenage years. I had a hard time imagining he was ever awkward, and I was sure he was exaggerating for my benefit. Again, I was struck by how easily the conversation flowed with him. There was nothing forced. When we finished eating, we carried our plates to the kitchen sink, rinsed them off, and loaded them into the dishwasher. He got even more points for helping with the cleanup.

When the dishwasher was loaded, Liam pulled me toward him and wrapped his arms around me. He ran his fingers through my hair, as goosebumps formed on every inch of my skin. I wanted so badly to give myself up to him, body and soul, but that voice was inside my head, nagging me the way it always did. I knew that it was too soon. I had to listen to my instincts.

As if sensing my withdrawal, Liam took a step back from me. He seemed to know my emotional state was fragile, and was trying hard not to push me.

"Well, I guess I had better get a move on. I have

some more work to get done today. I had a really great time last night, and this morning. Thank you for spending time with me."

"Thank you, Liam. Thanks for understanding and being patient with me. You're probably going to get tired of me and my hang-ups eventually, but I just want to say that no matter what happens, you're a really great guy. A lot of men would have taken advantage of me last night, but you were a real gentleman."

"You'll be surprised at how patient I can be, Emma, and I guarantee I am not going to get tired of you." Liam brushed my lips lightly with his.

After he left, I showered and got ready for work. I needed to place an order at the shop and take care of some paperwork.

"Back to reality," I said as I headed out the front door.

Chapter Eight

After leaving Emma's house, Liam headed to the library. He didn't have any more research to do today, but he wanted to talk to Sadie. He was going to need all the help he could get with Emma, and he decided to go the person who knew her best. He walked into the research room, and saw Sadie helping a library patron. She immediately noticed him and walked over.

"Hey there, how was the big date? I haven't talked to Em yet today, so I'll get the scoop from you first."

"It was great, actually. We had a really nice time. Emma is easy to talk to, which you already know. She's funny and caring and genuine. She also doubts herself a lot, which I'm hoping I can help her change. Another thing I learned is that she makes a great breakfast," Liam grinned mischievously.

"You were still there at breakfast? Does that mean you two...never mind, Emma will tell me later," Sadie trailed off.

"Well, I'm a gentleman, so I won't go into details, but no, it doesn't mean anything other than we talked a lot, and got to know each other better. And not in the way you're thinking. We just slept."

"Huh, what do you know? I think you've gotten to her." Sadie was amazed Emma had let her guard down so much. "If Emma let you spend the night, sex or not, then she is starting to trust you, which is something I never thought I would see."

"That's good, because I want her to trust me, Sadie. I know it's fast, and I haven't said this to Emma for fear of really scaring her, but I have serious feelings for her. I need to make her trust me, to see that I'm not going to hurt her."

"Want my advice? You need to take it slowly, and win her over. Let her see you're in it for the long haul. Emma is terrified of getting hurt again, and even more afraid of her girls getting hurt."

"I would never hurt them. I want to protect them, and make sure they're never hurt again."

"Wow, that's some pretty serious talk, Liam. Impressive."

Liam and Sadie chatted for several more minutes. By the time he left, Liam had a plan of action formulating in his brain.

Leaving the library, he decided he couldn't wait to see Emma again, even though it had only been a couple of hours. So he headed to Morning Glory. He stood outside of the coffee shop and watched Emma while she went about her work, talking and laughing with customers.

He thought back to how this had all started. At first, he wanted to simply become friends in the hopes of learning more about Jacob and his connection to Veronica. He hadn't meant to be deceitful. He simply knew Emma was a good source of information, and he had come to town to benefit from that connection. He felt a twinge of regret that his original intention had been to use her to get evidence. He hadn't considered for a minute he would fall for the woman. As soon as he saw her, though, he knew it was going to be more.

After learning about her life with Jacob, he was determined not to see her get hurt again. Emma had experienced so much pain and sadness in the past. He found himself wanting to make her happy. He was most definitely invested in her. If he had anything to do with it, she would never be hurt again.

Even though it wasn't part of the plan, he couldn't stay away. It was a dangerous game he was playing, and he was uncertain how it would all unfold.

He was still investigating Jacob and Veronica, and was as determined as ever to find answers. Yet, it was difficult to separate Emma and his feelings from the case. They were so intertwined there was no real way to differentiate between the two. He knew if he stood a chance with Emma she could never know about his connection to Jacob. She would never trust him again if she found out. Liam prayed that it didn't all blow up in his face.

***

I was pouring coffee for one of my customers when I looked up and saw Liam walking through the front door. I smiled as I noticed him. I went behind the counter, grabbed the coffee pot, and filled Liam's coffee mug.

"Long time no see." I handed him his cup, unable to comprehend it had only been a couple of hours since I saw him, but I had missed him already. I was such a goner.

"Yeah, I guess I couldn't stay away. I know, guys are supposed to be aloof and hard to get, but I can't seem to pull that off with you." Liam laughed.

"It's okay. I won't tell anyone and ruin your image. I don't like games either. I don't have time for them."

"Yeah, I can imagine you don't have a lot of extra time on your hands at all, with your girls and running a business. I'm not sure how you handle it all, and still manage to look so beautiful all the time." Liam smiled, sending chills down my spine.

"Well, I don't have a lot of choice in the matter. The girls and the shop need taken care of, so I just do it." I shrugged. "There's really no magic to it. I just keep putting one foot in front of the other every day and getting things done."

"I beg to differ. What I see you do daily is definitely magic. You take care of the shop, your friends, your home, and your daughters. What I want to know, Emma, is who takes care of you?" Liam asked, suddenly serious.

Caught off guard by the tone of his voice, I didn't know how to respond. I was amazed at the things he saw when he looked at me. I felt like he actually got me. He understood what made me tick. How many times had I wished that someone was there to take care of me?

Sometimes it weighed so heavily on me. It was hard being everything to everyone. Sometimes I didn't know how I kept it all going. It really was exhausting, and if I dwelled on it too much, it was overwhelming.

"Well, I guess I take care of myself," I answered evenly, not sure what else to say.

About that time, Jane called me over with a question about an order. I told Liam I had to go. I noticed he had a strange look on his face as he watched me walk away.

Chapter Nine

I glanced at the clock and saw that it was already 3:30 in the afternoon. I had a running agreement with the girls' bus driver that if I wasn't standing in front of the house when she came, she could simply drop the girls off next door at Morning Glory. I smiled as they walked through the front door. They sat down at their favorite table. I went to the pastry cupboard and split a huge blueberry muffin three ways. I placed it in front of them as I kissed them all hello. They hungrily ate their snack while I finished up my work.

I was tired, and didn't even want to think of all of the chores waiting for me at home as I wiped down the tables. Lily jumped in and started stacking the chairs, and Dahlia washed the plates after they inhaled the muffin. We gathered our things, locked up, and headed home.

When we got inside, I told them to get homework started. With only a little bit of argument, they did as I said. I went into the laundry room and started a load. There always seemed to be a mountain of it, and if I missed one day, it multiplied quickly.

Laundry started, I went to the table to help Rose, who was struggling with a math problem. I could certainly sympathize with my daughter, who hated math. I hadn't enjoyed math as a child either. As an adult, I still wasn't fond of it. Like the laundry, though, it was a necessary evil.

I went to the refrigerator, wondering what I could make for dinner that was simple. I couldn't believe how burned out I felt. The last thing I wanted to do was cook. I was still looking in the refrigerator, waiting to be inspired, when the doorbell rang.

I went to the front door and opened it. To my surprise, there was a deliveryman from Chen's Chinese Garden standing there with a large box full of delicious-smelling food.

"Can I help you?" My brain was puzzled as to why he was at my front door.

"Is this 3321 State Street?" asked the deliveryman.

"Yes, it is, but there must be a mistake. I didn't order anything."

"Is your name Emma McCoy?"

"It is. I'm still a little confused." I was not sure what was going on.

"Well, this food is for you. There's a note attached that might explain it, but it's all yours." He handed the box to me. "No need for a tip, it's already been taken care of."

"Thank you," I called to the man as he headed down the porch steps.

I took the box into the kitchen and sat it on the counter. I opened it up, and on top of the food was a note. Intrigued, I opened it.

Emma, you seemed really tired today, and I wanted to make your night a little easier. I hope you like Chinese food. Yours, Liam.

I couldn't believe what I was seeing. Was this guy for real? He had thought ahead, knowing how tired I had been earlier. He had taken something off of my list of tasks, making my night a bit easier. He was such a thoughtful man. I had never known anyone quite like him. He really was making it hard for me to take things slowly.

The girls looked up from their homework when they saw the box of Chinese food, and let out a loud cheer. I told them that Liam had sent it.

"Liam is really nice, Mom," Rose said.

"Yeah, Mom, I think you should go out on another date with him." Dahlia laughed.

"You're awfully quiet, Lily." I turned to my oldest daughter, uncertain how she felt about me dating. "What do you think of Liam?"

"He seems nice. He's not like a lot of other guys," Lily said quietly. "I guess it's okay if you want to date him."

"Well, I'm glad I have your approval, because you know we're a team." I hugged Lily closely, wanting her to know that her opinion truly mattered to me. "I won't do anything that you aren't ready for. I don't exactly know what's going on with me and Liam, but I do know that he is really thoughtful, and I like him a lot." I realized that no matter how hard I tried to fight it, it was the truth. "I think I might like to spend more time with him." I searched my older daughters' faces for more clues. I needed to be certain that they were okay with this. Dahlia smiled at me happily, and for once, Lily didn't have a look of concern on her face.

"Let's eat Chinese food!" Rose interrupted my thoughts.

After dinner, I cleaned up the kitchen and settled the girls down for the night. I gave them strict instructions to do some reading in their beds before I came to tuck them in. While they were reading, I took the laundry from the washer and put it into the dryer, all the while thinking of Liam. I wondered what he was doing right now. How did he spend his evenings? He seemed to be in my thoughts constantly these days.

An hour later, the laundry was done, the girls were tucked in and asleep, and I retreated to my room to get ready for bed. After undressing and removing my makeup, I hopped into bed and grabbed my phone. I debated on whether I should call Liam or text him. Deciding that such a nice gesture deserved a phone call, I dialed his number. The phone rang only one time before Liam picked it up.

"Hey, Emma."

The sound of his voice alone was enough to make my heart beat a little faster. His voice was deep and smooth and glided across me like silk. It made me feel giddy, like a teenager in love for the first time. I couldn't believe the reaction that I had to him. It was really hard to fathom he could have such an effect on me.

"Hi, Liam," I replied, trying hard not to give my reaction away. "I had to call you. What you did today, with the Chinese food, was one of the nicest things anyone has ever done for me. It was more thoughtful than you know. It was a relief to have that one thing taken off of my to-do list for tonight."

"I'm glad I could help. You take care of everyone all of the time. I just thought someone should take care of you for once."

"It was nice to not have to think about cooking dinner for a change." I laughed. "That's sort of my least favorite part of the day."

"So, what are you doing right now?"

"Well, I'm sitting in my bed talking to you."

"Um, what are you wearing?" Liam's voice lowered seductively.

"You don't even want to know." I giggled, looking down at my threadbare pajamas. "It's very unsexy."

"Anything on you is sexy, Emma."

My heart began racing. How could he do this to me with only his words?

"So when do I get to see you again?"

"Well, what do you have in mind?" I was pretty much up for anything at this point, as long as it meant being near him.

"I was thinking I would take you and the girls out for dinner and a movie on Friday. What do you think?"

I was surprised. He was not only asking me out, but including my children as well. My heart melted. This was not an ordinary man. He had figured out that the way to my heart was through my girls, and he was playing his hand well.

"Yes, I would like that. I'm pretty sure the girls would too. Do you like princess movies? Because I haven't watched a movie without princesses in ten years,"

I warned.

"Princesses are my favorite." Liam laughed, sending chills down my spine. We continued to talk, and before I knew it, an hour had passed. I knew I had better get some rest if I had any hopes of productivity tomorrow.

"I need to get some sleep now. Thank you again for dinner."

"It was my pleasure," Liam replied. "By the way, I'll probably come in and see you tomorrow. After all, tomorrow is only Thursday and I seem to have this need to see you every day."

"I hope you do, because Friday seems awfully far away. Night Liam." I hung up the phone.

I turned off the bedside lamp and snuggled beneath my blankets. Today had been a good day. Thoughts of Liam swirled in my mind, filling me with anticipation for Friday night.

Chapter Ten

In the darkness, the man, dressed completely in black, waited and watched. He sat in his car, lights turned off to avoid being noticed, and he plotted. It had taken him quite some time to find her, but now that he had, it was only a matter of time. He had hit the jackpot by discovering where she lived. Sitting outside of Emma's house was his new favorite pastime.

He knew she had the answers he needed. He had followed her for months, without her knowledge. He had watched her, observing her movements and habits and waiting for the right time. Emma was a very predictable woman. It was an added bonus her home and business were side by side. It made surveillance that much easier. He knew the time was coming soon, and when it did, he was going to make her tell him all of her secrets. Emma was the only one who had the answers.

Glancing toward the lovely Victorian house, he saw the upstairs light go off. Good, she was probably falling asleep, feeling warm and safe in her bed.

His eyes never leaving the dark rectangle, he waited. He was a patient man. He had to be. Impatience usually spelled disaster in his line of work. His occupation had taught him that "good things come to those who wait." He had learned to bide his time to get what he wanted.

"Enjoy your security while you can, Emma. You won't have it for long," said the man as he started the car's engine and drove off into the night.

Chapter Eleven

I was awakened by the buzzing of my alarm the next morning. Fumbling around on the bedside table, I found the button and turned it off. Taking a moment to stretch and to fully awaken, my first thoughts of the morning were centered on Liam. I thought back to last night, and the wonderful dinner arrangements he had made. He certainly seemed to be surprising me at every turn. He was definitely not what I had expected him to be. He always seemed to be concerned for my well-being, and genuinely appeared to care how I was feeling, even if there was nothing in it for him.

I thought about my relationship with Jacob, and realized Liam was of completely different stock than my late husband. Jacob had only been interested in me taking care of him. He would never have thought of doing something nice for me for the sole purpose of making my day easier. Being around Liam was a whole new experience for me, and one I was quickly learning to enjoy. It scared me a little bit to think of how attached I was getting to him, though.

Quickly showering and dressing for the day, I headed down to the kitchen. While the coffee was brewing, I went to the front porch to get the morning paper.

I felt unusually cheerful and chipper this morning. Maybe it had something to do with Liam and our upcoming date? An hour later, I sent three very happy girls off to school with full tummies. I loaded the dishwasher, finished cleaning the kitchen, and made a spur of the moment decision that I was going to take a day for myself. It had been quite some time since I had skipped work, and Jane would be more than happy to cover for me. She was always telling me I needed some down time, and for once, I was going to listen. I picked up the phone and called next door. As expected, Jane was pleased to hear that I would not be in today.

"Well, I have the day off. Now, what do I do?" I asked myself. "Maybe I need a new outfit for tomorrow's date."

Deciding on a course of action, I opted for walking to the local boutique. The day was perfect for a nice leisurely stroll downtown. Grabbing my purse, I headed out the front door.

Trés Chic, Beckland's nicest clothing store, was about five blocks from my house. I couldn't remember the last time I had gone shopping for myself. I was always buying things for the girls, but never really spent much money on myself. I loved the way clothes looked on others, but was never satisfied with how they looked on me. I didn't really have the knack for picking out things that complimented my shape. I basically lived in jeans and T-shirts, and very rarely dressed up. I wasn't sure what had come over me, but the prospect of a new outfit put an extra spring in my step.

I said hello to a couple of neighborhood friends as I headed to the boutique. My friends and neighbors must have had the same thought as me, because people took advantage of the great weather and walked into town or worked in their yards. I was grateful for the change of pace, and happy to have a day off.

I was almost to the boutique when I got the strangest sensation I was being followed. Turning to look behind me, I saw a green sedan ease into a parking spot along the street. A man got out and put some change into the parking meter. I noticed that he was tall and looked rather intimidating. He looked around, as if trying to decide which direction to go.

I wasn't sure what struck me as odd about him, other than he was dressed completely in black on such a sunny spring day. The sunglasses were a given, still his presence made me uneasy. He seemed out of place to me. I didn't recognize him, and he didn't appear to be doing anything more than parking his car.

Despite the warm morning, I suddenly felt chilled. I glanced around to see where he was headed. Perhaps he was lost, as he didn't seem to have a destination in mind. Instead of heading into one of the stores, he stood beside his car, casually leaning on the hood. He pulled out his phone and dialed. I was just about to turn away when he looked my direction. He lowered his sunglasses and his icy stare made me shiver. I broke eye contact, not wanting him to think I was watching.

"Emma, you're just paranoid," I scolded myself. Maybe I was paranoid, but something about the exchange had made me quite anxious. Laughing nervously, I pushed the nagging thought aside and walked into the trendy boutique to see what I could find.

"Hey, Emma," said Nora, the owner of Trés Chic. "I haven't seen you in a while. How have you been?"

"Hi, Nora, I'm great! The shop looks good. It's been so long since I've been in here I forgot how fabulous this place is." Giddy with anticipation, I browsed, taking in the trendy clothing. I fingered a silk blouse, wondering if I could pull off something so fancy. It had been some time since I'd bought something for myself.

"Are you after something special, or just looking around?"

"Well, I'm not really sure what I'm looking for, actually. It was sort of a spur of the moment decision for me. I took the day off and decided I need a new outfit."

"Casual or dressy?"

"Well, casual, but kind of, well, sexy I guess," I said quickly, slightly embarrassed.

"Well, with your curves, sweetie, you can definitely pull off sexy," Nora gave me a conspiratorial wink. "Just leave it to me. You're such a knockout; you're going to make my job a piece of cake. Trust me."

"Okay, but I haven't done sexy in a really long time, so go easy on me." I laughed, already nervous about how the clothes would look on me.

I always thought Nora had a keen eye for fashion, and was so impeccably dressed. She led me into a dressing room. Despite my apprehension, I trusted her taste implicitly.

"I'll be back in a minute with some things for you to try on." She disappeared into the clothing racks.

I waited nervously. I wasn't used to having the focus on me, and it made me a bit uncomfortable. What was I thinking, anyway? I'm a mom. I couldn't pull off sexy anymore. I was pretty sure that my days of being sensual were far behind me.

"Here, sweetie, start with these." Nora handed me a pair of jeans and a shirt. "And don't say no until you've tried them on."

I looked at the clothing she had handpicked for me. I would never have chosen these items for myself. Glancing at them and seeing they were much classier than my usual jeans and T-shirts, I decided to give Nora's expert opinion a chance.

I slid on the form-fitting jeans and black low-cut blouse. Looking at myself in the mirror, I decided the effect wasn't half bad. It was definitely more daring than I was used to, but, I had to admit, I actually liked the way the garments hugged my curves. I was impressed with Nora's ability to pick out the perfect outfit on the first try.

"Nora, you're a genius," I called through the dressing room door. "I'll take the whole outfit. Can you recommend some shoes too?"

"I have the perfect pair of size eights waiting for you at the counter." She laughed, sounding quite pleased with herself.

A few minutes later, I had the jeans, blouse, and flowered wedges she picked out stashed in my shopping bag. Feeling happy with my purchases, I headed for home. I was daydreaming about Liam, not paying attention to my surroundings when I saw the green car from earlier driving slowly behind me. Was the driver following me, or was it just a coincidence? I decided it was just my overactive imagination. Arriving home, I went inside, oblivious that the driver lingered outside far longer than I would have been comfortable with.

Chapter Twelve

At six o'clock the next evening, I stood in my bedroom putting the finishing touches on my appearance. The jeans and blouse looked amazing, and the flowered shoes added a touch of whimsy. I knew that I looked good. I heard the doorbell ring, hurried downstairs, and rushed to open the door. Liam had gone casual tonight, with faded jeans and a polo shirt, but he was just as handsome as ever.

"Hey, gorgeous." Liam smiled, as he handed me a beautiful bouquet of red roses. "I brought you these."

"Thank you." I smiled, blushing a little at his compliment. "Looks like you still have something behind your back. What's the secret?"

"You already got yours. Where are the girls?"

About that time, Lily, Dahlia, and Rose came running down the stairs.

"Well, hello girls."

"Hi, Liam," the girls replied as one.

Rose ran forward and gave Liam a big hug. He had become her hero since rescuing her.

"I have something for you, Rose." Liam reached into a bag and handed her a small dog. "I hope you like stuffed animals."

"I *love* them. How did you know dogs are my favorite?"

"Just a good guess." Liam laughed.

Dahlia and Lily weren't quite so exuberant, but they both smiled politely watching Liam and Rose.

"I didn't forget you two. Dahlia, I got you the new Cammy Cooper book. I heard it was what all the girls are reading, and it just came out today. I hope you like it." Liam handed the book to Dahlia.

"I have been waiting ages for this! Mom said she would take me to the bookstore this weekend, but now she doesn't have to! Thank you, Liam." Dahlia beamed, running her fingers over the cover of the book.

"Lily, I got you some flowers, too. I figured that a lady always likes flowers." Liam handed the bouquet of pink roses to Lily.

"Um, no one has ever bought me flowers before," Lily said shyly, breathing in the scent of them. "Thanks, Liam."

Lily and I headed into the kitchen to put our flowers into some water. When we returned, Liam, Dahlia, and Rose were engaged in a very serious conversation about our movie choice for this evening.

"So, girls, what are we seeing tonight? I thought we could go for pizza before the movie if that's okay?"

"That's fine with us. We're always hungry." Dahlia giggled.

"Mom said maybe we could see the new Princess Mysteries movie. I'll bet that doesn't sound too fun to you, though," Lily said.

"Well, don't tell anyone, but I've seen all of the Princess Mysteries. My niece loves them, and I always take her. That's why I'm her favorite uncle."

"Aren't you her only uncle?" I smiled.

"That's beside the point," Liam answered with a grin.

"I guess I didn't expect you to know what they were," Lily added.

"I'm full of surprises." Liam looked my way.

We all piled into my SUV and headed to Pete's Pizza. We gorged ourselves until I was sure the girls were literally going to burst, and then headed to City Center Cinema. Liam got our tickets for the show, and we headed into the darkened theater. Ninety fun-filled minutes later, the movie was over and we headed happily for home, with the theme song of the Princess Mysteries stuck in my head.

I couldn't believe how wonderfully the night had gone. Liam was funny and interesting, and the girls had taken to him right away. He included them in the conversation, and gave them the attention they needed. I even saw Rose grab his hand when we were walking to the car earlier. The girls were usually cautious of strangers, especially men, but that was not the case with Liam. I couldn't believe how easy it all felt. It was almost as if we had been together for years. There was a laidback comradery between us and my girls were as smitten with him as I was.

Arriving at home, we made our way inside. I instructed the girls to go straight upstairs, get into their pajamas, get their teeth brushed, and be ready for their tuck-in. Liam stood awkwardly by the front door, not sure if he should come in or go. I decided to make things easy for him.

"Make yourself comfortable. I'll get the girls into bed and we can have some tea or something."

"Sure. Can I help with anything?"

"No, I've got this down." I laughed as I directed him toward the living room.

He settled himself on the couch, seeming quite at ease in my home. It felt nice having him here. I headed upstairs to tuck the girls in. After successfully completing that task, I returned downstairs.

"Liam, the girls would like for you to come upstairs and tell them goodnight if that's okay," I said shyly, not sure how he might respond.

"Sure, I'd like that." He headed upstairs, stopping in the doorway of each girl's room to say goodnight. I heard Rose thank him for the stuffed animal, and Lily said she appreciated the flowers. I was expecting Dahlia to thank him for the book, but instead, she teased him for liking "girl" movies. Liam took it all in stride and laughed happily as he defended his manhood to my eight-year-old daughter. I giggled at their exchange.

He found me in the kitchen, putting the tea kettle

onto the stove. Settling himself at the counter, he watched me work.

"Emma, you have amazing girls. You must be very proud."

"I am. They are wonderful. I don't know what I would do without them. They really seem quite taken with you." I turned giving him a huge smile, happy he seemed to really care about them in such a short time.

"The feeling's mutual. I'm also quite taken with their mother," Liam said, walking across the kitchen to where I was standing.

He leaned down and kissed me. My response was immediate and heated. I wrapped my arms around his neck, and melted into him. I knew that I had serious feelings for him. He had been so patient with me, and all of my quirks hadn't bothered him a bit. He had broken down my walls a brick at a time. I loved how I felt when I was with him, but watching how great he was with the girls made me realize I needed to give this a chance. I knew I was no longer able to resist, so I didn't.

Breaking away from Liam, I headed over to the stove and turned off the burner. I knew where things were headed, and I was ready. I walked back, took his hand, and led him upstairs to my room. Instead of the nerves I usually felt, there was nothing but confidence. I knew this wasn't a rushed decision made in the heat of the moment. I wanted to be with Liam, and I had never been more certain of anything in my life.

Once we were inside, I locked the door. Tonight there would be no turning back. Walking over to Liam, I pulled his head down toward mine. Our mouths met. He brushed my lips lightly with his own at first, but I was hungry for him. I pressed my mouth hard against his, desperate to let him know how much I wanted him. Wrapping my arms around his neck, I pulled him closer. He engulfed me in the strong circle of his embrace. I had never felt as safe as I did in that moment with Liam.

There was no way I could extinguish the fire he ignited inside of me, and I honestly didn't want to. I had tried to withhold myself from him. I had tried not to let him in. Despite my best efforts, he had gotten beneath my skin. His kindness and patience had endeared him to me. I knew that I was making this decision with my eyes wide open. I was no longer afraid. I trusted him in a way that I had never experienced. I felt alive with Liam, more alive than I ever had before. I felt like I was waking up from a long sleep. With Liam, I felt complete.

Chapter Thirteen

I awakened the next morning, my limbs entwined with Liam's. I blushed a little thinking of last night. It had been wonderful... Sometimes decisions made in the heat of passion can be regretted in the light of day. Surprisingly, I didn't feel that way at all, which convinced me even further what we had was a good thing. I wasn't sure where we would go from here, but decided to take it one day at a time.

"Morning," Liam said sleepily, snuggling closer to me.

"Morning." I smiled. "You're welcome to stay here, but any minute I am going to have three girls knocking on the door wondering why it's locked. I need to get up."

"Okay. Do you mind if I take a quick shower?"

"Sure, go right ahead and make yourself at home. There are clean towels in the cupboard. I'll go make some coffee and breakfast."

I headed down to the kitchen to get the coffee started. I decided on waffles, and got out the ingredients. I wasn't quite sure how I was going to explain Liam's presence here this morning, but I would figure that out when I needed to. I was "flying by the seat of my pants" as they say, and didn't know how this was all going to play out.

When the waffles were finished, I called the girls downstairs. They were excited when they saw I had made one their favorite breakfasts. I fixed each girl a plate and soon everyone was devouring the fluffy goodness.

"These are yummy, Mama," Rose said, with her mouth full.

"Thank you, sweetie, but how about you finish chewing before you talk." I leaned down to give her a kiss on the top of her head. She was so cute she melted my heart.

The girls finished breakfast, took their plates to the sink, and headed upstairs. Sadie was due any minute to pick them up for a shopping trip they had planned. She was so good about giving me a break every now and then. I glanced at the stairs, wondering where Liam was. A couple of minutes later, my daughters ran back downstairs just as the doorbell rang. I opened the front door for Sadie.

"Morning, Em. You're looking chipper. How was your date?" Sadie asked, looking at me suspiciously.

"It was great. We all had a great time." I was not sure how to give her the scoop that I knew she was after with the girls standing right there.

"So many things left unsaid... Guess you'll have to fill me in later. These girlies and I have shopping to do." She kissed me on the cheek with a pointed look and herded the girls out the front door. She knew me so well, and that I was obviously hiding something.

Entering the kitchen, I saw Liam helping himself to a plate of waffles.

"I thought maybe you got lost in the shower." I laughed.

"Well, I actually just waited upstairs until I heard the girls leave. I wasn't sure you were ready to explain me being here in the morning quite yet."

"That was really thoughtful of you. I wasn't really ready, and it could have been awkward. Thank you for being so considerate of the girls' feelings." Not wanting there to be so much space between us, I sat down next to him and planted a kiss on his mouth.

"I could definitely get used to this every day," Liam mumbled between kisses. "It doesn't get much better than waffles and kissing a beautiful woman first thing in the morning."

"Well, I aim to please, Mr. O'Reilly." I was feeling practically giddy with delight.

"I'm thinking that since you made breakfast, I'll

clean the kitchen while you shower and get ready for work. It's the least I can do,"

"Deal," I said, kissing him quickly before heading upstairs.

***

Liam cleaned the countertops and stove, and then loaded the dishwasher. Emma was an amazing woman. They fit together, as if they had always known one another. He could definitely see a future with her, and her girls. A family had been near impossible with his job and never finding the right woman, but with Emma his dream of having a family seemed within reach. He had been warring with himself since he first saw her not to get too involved. He obviously threw that idea right out the window.

His entire life had been spent questioning everything. His skepticism and ability to remain detached were the two things that made him good at his job. The other thing that made him an expert in his field was good instincts. His gut told him Emma was the one for him. He was pretty sure she felt the same, but with her past, he wasn't going to push. He would be patient and let her set the pace.

However, the nagging thought in the back of his mind, needing to come clean to Emma, overshadowed his fledgling happiness. Did she know about Jacob's checkered past? Was it possible for a wife to have absolutely no idea that her husband was harboring such a secret? She had never mentioned his involvement in the jewelry theft, but, he had always assumed she was aware of it. Now that he knew her, he doubted his initial assumption. She obviously knew of his affair, but he was pretty sure she was clueless as to Jacob's true nature.

He was not ready for Emma to learn he had been investigating Jacob. To Liam's dismay, the investigation was completely stalled at the moment. He had been hopeful when he moved to Beckland, sure that the answers he was searching for were here with Emma. Since his arrival, though, no new evidence had turned up. Despite his original idea, Emma had not been a useful resource as far as the case was concerned.

Liam considered himself to be a moral and ethical man, and as such, truly wanted to tell Emma the whole story. If he told her, though, she might panic and think he was just trying to get close to her to find out more about her late husband. Granted, that had been the case in the beginning, but had all changed once he got to know her.

In all truth, Liam was attracted to her from the first time he laid eyes on her six years ago. The closer they became, the less he thought about Jacob and his duty.

He was in love with Emma. That made him pause. It should be too soon, but he trusted his gut. When it felt right, he went with it. For the time being, Liam decided on the path of least resistance, opting to keep his secret a little longer. The odds of her finding out were slim, and he didn't want to risk their future. No, he wouldn't tell her. He prayed to God that he was making the right choice.

Chapter Fourteen

Things moved along well the next couple of months. Liam and I were inseparable. He joined the girls and me each night for dinner. He stayed over, but left in the mornings before the girls woke up. We weren't trying to be secretive; I just wanted to be sure we were headed toward a future together before the girls understood the seriousness of our relationship.

The girls loved him, and had gotten used to him being around. Pleased with the way our relationship was progressing, I found I trusted him even more.

Tonight after work, Liam was grilling steaks for dinner. My grill was practically brand new, since I preferred to do my cooking inside. I was happy someone was getting some use out of it.

It was nice to have a man around. Yesterday, the kitchen sink was clogged. Normally, I would have picked up the phone and called a plumber, but Liam jumped in and had it working in no time. I wasn't used to being taken care of, and found myself enjoying and appreciating it.

I was preparing a salad when Liam came up behind me, wrapping his arms around me.

"I didn't even hear you come in," I said, pulling his head down so I could give him a kiss.

"I snuck in when you weren't looking." He laughed.

"Good thing you didn't surprise me too much, considering this sharp knife in my hand."

"How was your day?" He settled against the kitchen counter.

"It was busy, but good." I continued chopping vegetables, relishing in Liam's company.

"My day was good too," Liam said. "My furniture truck arrived, so it looks like I get to finally move in to my house."

"I can help unpack if you need it. You know, I

haven't even seen your house yet. You always come here."

"Once I'm unpacked, we will have dinner at my place," Liam's tone was one I had never heard before. Was it me, or did he seem uncomfortable? I assumed he would be happy to move in to his new house.

"The steaks are on the counter beside the fridge." I changed the subject and pointed across the room. "I marinated them all day, so they should be tasty."

Liam grabbed them and headed out back to the grill I had pre-heated. We invited Sadie to dinner, so we would have a full house. I had been looking forward to our get-together all day.

A few minutes later, she arrived. After asking me what she could do to help and me telling her to just go and relax, she joined Liam outside. Their banter reached through the open window.

"Hey, Liam. You look pretty good at that barbeque, like you're a professional."

"I am. Didn't Emma tell you?"

"Just make sure you don't burn the steaks."

Having finished things up in the kitchen, I went outside and joined them. I couldn't believe how good this felt. It was a perfect afternoon with my daughters, my favorite man, and my best friend. I would never have imagined myself at this point a few months ago. I was blissfully happy and thankful for this new feeling. I certainly didn't want to rush into things, but I could envision a future with Liam. I was having a hard time remembering how things were without him. In the span of a couple of months, he had become an integral part of my life.

"So, Liam, Emma mentioned a few moments ago your furniture has finally arrived and you're ready to start moving into your house," Sadie said, bringing me back to the moment.

"Yeah, it seemed like it would never happen, but

the house is ready and it looks like it's time."

Just then the home phone rang. I ran into the kitchen and picked it up on the third ring.

"Hello."

The sound of breathing met my greeting.

"Hello…is anyone there?" I repeated.

Still no answer, but the line was open and I could hear noise in the background.

"Hello…who is this?" I tried a third time. Suddenly, the line went dead.

I was not sure how long I stared at the receiver. My shaking hands as I hung up the phone revealed the tumult warring inside me. I was sure someone had been on the line. Worry creasing my brow, I headed back outside.

"That was strange. They didn't answer. I guess it was a wrong number. Probably a telemarketer." I shrugged, trying to convince myself it was no big deal. I looked toward Liam and Sadie for reassurance. They hadn't seemed to key in on my anxiety, so I decided to change the subject. I was obviously making something out of nothing.

"It looks like the steaks are done, huh?"

"Yep, girls, it's dinner time," Liam called.

Lily, Rose, and Dahlia came running. They had been playing, and apparently worked up an appetite.

"Great! I'm starving," Dahlia said, sitting down at the table.

"Me too," Rose added.

"I could definitely eat," Lily said.

Liam and I fixed their plates, working side by side in a sort of rhythm. I was amazed at how we had blended ourselves so quickly. He and I made a great team.

We dug into dinner, eating and talking happily, and I forgot about the strange phone call.

***

The man watching them through the backyard fence pulled his black ball cap a little further down over his eyes. He was pleased with how well his plan was coming together. He had laid all of the groundwork, and it was almost time for action. He could hardly wait until it all began. He loved feeling in control, and he knew that he held Emma's very future in his powerful hands.

Stupid, oblivious Emma was so engrossed in her family that she didn't even notice him. He watched her as she laughed at something her daughter said. He found himself quite obsessed with her. She was a beautiful woman, and he had been fantasizing about her a lot lately. That only fueled his fire all the more. He alternated between wanting to hurt her and wanting to be alone with her.

His mind raced with the many ways that he could wreak havoc on Emma's life. He reminded himself to be patient. There were moments when he could literally feel his sanity slipping through his fingers. He had to keep it together for just a little longer. If he acted without thinking, it would ruin everything. His plan hinged on the element of surprise. It wouldn't be long before he unleashed his fury. He took in the happy scene before him and felt his anger rise. Why should she get to be happy? He certainly wasn't. The man watched for a few minutes, snapped some pictures, then put his cellphone in his pocket and walked away.

Chapter Fifteen

After dinner was eaten and dishes were carried inside, Sadie and I began to clean up the kitchen. Liam settled himself in the living room on the couch with Rose on his lap. Dahlia and Lily were seated on either side of him while he read their favorite book, *Chloe the Ballerina*. Sadie watched them from the kitchen.

"They sure seem at home, don't they?" she said to me.

"Yeah, it's kind of amazing the way they are together. Lily was skeptical at first, but Liam won her over pretty quickly. It scares me a little bit, knowing how much we could all get hurt if this doesn't work out."

"Always the optimist." Sadie laughed.

"I know, I know, I'm trying. It's hard for me not to expect the worst, you know?"

"I know, Em. I really do understand. I just don't think Liam is that kind of guy. He seems pretty sincere with his feelings," Sadie continued. "He is so not like Jacob."

"No, I don't think he would purposely hurt us. That's not what I mean at all. It's just that...I don't know...I'm afraid of losing him now that I have him. I kept myself walled off for so long, and now that I've let him in, I keep getting these glimpses of what my life would be like without him. I don't like them at all, Sadie. I don't know how I would recover again." I said quietly, knowing I had finally hit on the truth of the matter.

"Faith, Em. Try and have a little faith. I really think things are going to turn out okay for you guys." Sadie gave me a quick hug. When I heard Sadie say it out loud, somehow it sounded as if it might just be true.

"Thanks, Sadie. You always have known how to say the right thing to me."

"Well, I'm beat, and I have to be up early for work tomorrow. I think I'm going to head home." Sadie kissed me on the cheek.

She said goodbye to the girls, and Liam, and then I walked her to the front door. I gave her a quick hug before she headed up the outside stairs to her apartment. As I looked toward the living room, I saw Liam on my couch and the girls playing happily on the floor below him. It was such a sweet, contented picture. It looked like a portrait of a cheerful family. I said a quick prayer that happiness had finally come to stay.

***

Liam looked around his house as he finished unpacking the last box. He had been working on getting settled in his new house for over a week now. He was happier than he had ever been in his life. He was determined to hold on to that happiness at all cost.

He had been so hopeful when he bought this house several months ago. When he had learned that Veronica Smith's home was up for sale in Beckland, he knew he had to jump on it. Rumor was that she had a hidden room in her house where she had stashed the jewelry. The only way to find out was to get inside the house. What better way to do that than to purchase it for himself? He had enough seniority in the department that he could work his cases from anywhere. Chicago was a quick plane trip from Beckland, so he could come and go in the office as he needed. Buying the house was pretty much a no-brainer in his opinion.

So far, he hadn't found any clues that led him to believe the jewelry was hidden here. Of course, he had been distracted with unpacking and moving in, but he had been hoping that finding them would be simple. He was wrong. Nothing about this case had ever been simple. He shouldn't expect it to be any different now. If anything, it was just getting more complicated as his involvement with Emma deepened.

He was uncomfortable about tonight. Seeing

Veronica's house and the house she lived in with Jacob was sure to make bad memories resurface for Emma. She had been asking a lot of questions, wondering when she could see the house. Of course, that was a normal reaction for a girlfriend to have. The secret he kept was anything but normal, though. Knowing he couldn't stall any longer, he had asked her over for dinner this evening, steering them toward dangerous territory. Emma's reaction to him living in her late husband's girlfriend's house was something he was not looking forward to.

Emma's past was a painful one. He didn't want to be responsible for causing her suffering, but he didn't know what else to do. He couldn't keep her away from his home forever without raising questions. Tonight would either make or break their budding relationship. He didn't know what he would do without Emma, and he hoped he never had to find out.

Chapter Sixteen

I was hurrying around trying to get the girls ready to spend the night upstairs with Sadie. As usual, they were looking forward to a night of girl time. I'm not sure what all they did up there, but the girls always came home with some fancy new nail polish or their hair fixed in creative ways. Sadie was the perfect aunt. She had graciously agreed to watch the girls so that Liam and I could have a quiet evening at his new place.

The two of us were having our first dinner there. He had done all of the moving in himself, and hadn't taken me up on my offer to help. I was pretty sure he was just being considerate and not wanting to ask me to do extra work.

For some reason, I couldn't figure out why, I had a nervous feeling in the pit of my stomach. Things were going so well. The girls were happy, and I was ecstatic. I couldn't remember the last time I had felt so completely taken care of. Liam was truly the "knight in shining armor" type. He was thoughtful, considerate, and he took my breath away with his romantic ways. Everything was perfect—so why couldn't I shake the feeling something was about to go wrong? I guess I was just a born pessimist. I was honestly trying, though.

"Come on girls! We need to head up to Sadie's. Bring your stuff downstairs please," I called upstairs.

Lily, Dahlia, and Rose ran down the stairs, overnight bags in hand. As excited as they were to stay at Sadie's, they didn't need to be told twice to hurry up. The girls and I headed out our door, and up the stairs to Sadie's. She answered before we even knocked. I wasn't sure who was more excited, Sadie or the girls.

"Be good for Sadie," I told my daughters, as I kissed each of them. "I will see you all tomorrow morning before school."

I thanked Sadie, gave them all a quick hug, and then

went back inside my house to finish getting dressed before Liam arrived.

I headed to my bedroom. I looked through my closet, deciding on casual attire tonight. After all, we were eating in, and that didn't require fancy clothes, thank goodness. I was curious about where he lived. I often wondered what type of place he would have, and I pictured him living in a very masculine home. He hadn't really talked much about it, and was pretty vague when I asked questions. Come to think of it, he wasn't very forthcoming with most questions I asked about his life before me. I didn't think he was purposely being secretive, but I was learning he didn't enjoy talking about himself. I certainly would love to know more about him and his past.

He told me he was close to his family, who all lived in Chicago. He had one sister, and two nieces, whom he absolutely adored. He was excited for us to meet them, and we had already made plans to make a trip there with the girls over the summer. I knew he hadn't had a lot of serious relationships and he didn't usually open up much with people. I was sure this was a result of his occupation. It was probably one of the reasons why he was such a great detective. Other than that, he'd said little about his life. Liam told me several times that nothing else mattered before he met me. Under any other circumstances, this would have made me nervous and uncomfortable, but I trusted him completely, and was certain he wasn't hiding anything from me.

I grabbed my favorite jeans and the new emerald green blouse I bought last week. Liam liked me in green, so when I saw the blouse in the store window I knew I had to have it. I liked that he was generous with his compliments. It boosted my ego and made me feel wanted. I never had to wonder where I stood with Liam, and I appreciated that about him. It took a lot of the usual guesswork out of our relationship.

I had just finished dressing when I heard the front door open and shut. I smiled to myself. Liam didn't knock anymore. I was happy that he felt comfortable at my house.

"I'm upstairs! I'll be right down," I called loudly.

I headed downstairs and found Liam putting the milk carton back into the refrigerator. I didn't notice a glass, and had the sudden realization that he had taken a drink directly out of the carton. He was such a guy, but he was my guy.

I walked up behind him, wrapping my arms around him. His muscles rippled beneath his shirt. My pulse immediately quickened. He turned around and encircled me in his arms. He bent down and hungrily claimed my mouth. I responded eagerly, as I always did. It was perfect with us. There was so much passion. I sometimes had a hard time containing it all. I had never had a relationship where there was so much give and take, in equal measure.

Liam tangled his fingers into my hair. He bent down and picked me up, sitting me on the counter in front of him. He was so strong. I was definitely not a small woman, but he lifted me and moved me as if I were.

"At this rate, we aren't going to make it to your house for dinner." I giggled in between kisses.

"That's okay. The house isn't going anywhere," Liam said, gently biting my earlobe.

"I know, but I do want to see it. The girls are at Sadie's for the night. Maybe we can continue this conversation there."

"If that's what you want." Liam helped me down from the counter. I sensed a bit of disappointment and anxiety in him. I wasn't sure what that was about. I assumed Liam would be happy to show me his new place. Maybe I was just imagining something that wasn't there.

"All right, baby, your wish is my command." He flashed me a smile that didn't quite reach his eyes.

We headed out and got into his car. Backing out of

my driveway, he headed down Main Street, drove a couple of blocks, and then he turned left onto Russell Street. It was a beautiful night, and I was enjoying the drive through town. We drove past Vinnie's, and I smiled thinking of our first date. We had certainly come a long way in two months.

Liam continued on Russell Street and took a right onto Briar Avenue. About this time, I felt the first prickle of uneasiness. We were headed toward the area of town where Jacob and I used to live. I usually avoided that part of town like the plague. There were too many bad memories there. It was when he turned off of Briar Avenue and onto Rosemary Lane that my palms began to sweat. I was fully convinced that Liam must be lost. That had to be it. What were the odds that his new house was on the same street where Jacob and I had lived? That would be too unbelievable to be true.

Liam glanced over at me, and I was sure he noticed how tense I was. I clenched my hands into fists, and I stared blankly out the window. He must have been confused by my behavior, but he didn't say anything. I wasn't sure that I could even form the words to explain my thoughts to him. I just kept staring out the window, hoping I could keep it together until he figured out where he was going.

I couldn't believe Liam had gotten lost in my old neighborhood. There was so much anxiety at being here again I couldn't even help him navigate. I closed off inside myself, feeling things I had avoided, and hadn't felt in a very long time. Being in this neighborhood gave me a sense of being locked in a dark room, knowing there was no way out. Tension rose inside me, and my stomach clenched tight as a fist as a feeling of dread arose in me.

"Sweetie, are you okay? You're pretty quiet."

"Yeah, I'm okay." I lied, barely even able to form words as my pulse quickened even more.

He headed to the end of Rosemary Lane and turned into a driveway. I let out an audible gasp. There had to be some mistake. This couldn't be his house.

"What are we doing here?" My voice rising with the panic inside of me as my worst fears came to life in front of me.

"This is my house, Emma."

"This can't be your house. This must be some cruel joke. It doesn't make any sense," I said quickly, wringing my hands in desperation.

"Emma, talk to me. Tell me what's wrong."

"This house..." I began, but then realized that I couldn't go on.

I had to get out of the car. I felt like I was suffocating. I needed air. I fumbled for the door handle, and practically leaped out of the passenger seat. I didn't know what to do. My first thought was to take off for home. I wanted to run from these emotions I didn't want to feel. I thought I had buried them deep inside of me, but here they were, rising like a phoenix from the ashes. I needed to get away from this place. I paced like a caged animal in the driveway beside the car.

I looked at the house. Slowly, I glanced to the left. There was the house I lived in with Jacob. It was just a house, nothing more, but it was so completely tied up in memories of hurt and betrayal that even looking at it put me right back in that place I had fought so hard to get away from. So many memories came flooding back. In that instant, they were far too real, and as much an open wound as if they had happened yesterday.

At the top of the pile were the emotions I had felt when I discovered Jacob and Veronica's affair. I felt it again, at that moment, the gut-wrenching pain of being betrayed. I had lived in that house for years with Jacob. We had shared a family and a life, and it was all a lie. Veronica had lived next door to us, pretending to be my friend, all the time sleeping with my husband. Wave after wave of emotion overtook me, and I collapsed on the driveway and started to sob.

It was obvious Liam wasn't sure what to do with me. He stood back for a couple of minutes, giving me space and allowing me to break down. Then he approached and sat down next to me on the driveway, cradling my sobbing body in his arms. I continued to weep for several minutes. I had never broken down quite like this. I had cried when I found out about the affair. I had cried when I buried Jacob, and realized my daughters no longer had a father. I had cried when my parents died, leaving me once again alone. But through all of those things, I had never fully allowed myself to fall apart. I had always kept it under control.

Now, I wept for all of the times I hadn't. I wept for the times I had been stronger than I wanted to be. I sat in the driveway, engulfed in Liam's strong arms and I cried harder than I had ever cried in all my life. It was as if someone had opened the floodgates, and now I didn't know how to close them. I cried until I couldn't cry anymore. When I finally ran out of tears, I wiped my eyes with my hands and looked at Liam.

I'm positive that he thought I was a complete mental case. What kind of woman had a nervous breakdown in the driveway of her boyfriend's new home? I wasn't sure what to say to him, but I had to say something.

"So, you're probably wondering why I went into hysterics in your new driveway."

"I'm thinking there must be a very good reason, and I'm hoping you'll fill me in," Liam said quietly.

"Liam…this house…your house is where Veronica Smith lived. The woman that was sleeping with my husband right under my nose. And," my voice quivered and I had to pause to gain some control, "the house beside it," I pointed to the left, "was where I lived with Jacob." I looked at it now and couldn't believe I had ever lived that life. I didn't like the woman I used to be. She was weak and too scared to take control of her life. I would never be that woman again.

I took a deep, shuddering breath and pulled myself up. Now that I was a bit calmer, I felt self-conscious that I had lost my composure in front of Liam. He hadn't seemed to mind, though, and simply held on to me while I broke down. He was his usual steady self, and that saw me through my worst fears.

"I'm sorry, Liam. I am sure this wasn't how you had envisioned tonight."

"Don't apologize to me, Emma. Don't ever think you have to apologize for your feelings." Liam pulled me close to him, his proximity doing wonders for my frazzled nerves.

"We don't have to stay. I can take you home and you never have to come back here again. I'll sell this house and buy another one. I never want to see you hurt like that again."

"No, I need to do this. I think it will be good for me to try and get past it. Can we go inside?" I asked, taking a deep breath.

"Only if you're sure." Liam continued to hold me close, concern written all over his face.

"I'm sure, Liam. Will you please show me your home?" I replied, sounding stronger than I actually felt.

He took my hand and we walked up the driveway to the front door, and Liam turned and looked at me. I suddenly felt extremely self-conscious. My makeup had to be smeared on my face, my eyes had to have been red and swollen from all of the crying, and I must have looked just awful. The way he looked at me made me unsure as to what he was thinking. It was a strange look; one I had never seen before.

"Emma, I have something to say," Liam said

90

hesitantly.

"Liam, I don't know if I can take any more revelations tonight. If it's something bad, maybe you can just keep it to yourself a bit longer." I laughed nervously.

"It's not bad. At least I don't think it's bad," Liam said, beginning to pace nervously on his front porch. My stomach felt like a million butterflies were having a heyday inside of me.

"Emma, I don't know if this is the right time or not, but I need to tell you something. From the first moment I saw you, something happened to me. I'm not usually the guy who rushes into things, but I can't seem to stop myself with you. I think you've bewitched me or something, and I'm not sure if I like it or not." He continued to pace.

My heart raced inside of my chest. I wasn't sure where he was going with this confession. Was he going to tell me that we were moving too fast and needed to back off? Was he breaking up with me?

He continued, "I don't know how to say what I want to say. I'm not even making any sense. Emma, I have loved you from the first time I laid eyes on you. I love the way you keep me on my toes, I love the way you are with your girls, I love how dedicated you are to your work, I love the way you made me work to win you over. I love the way you twirl your hair when you're nervous. I love the way you cry at the end of movies, and I love the way you make me feel like I can do anything. I love you."

I thought I might faint. Was I ready for love? If I was honest with myself, Liam was saying out loud the way I had been feeling about him for weeks. We both knew we were headed to this place and whether I was ready or not, I felt the same way.

"Emma, I said I love you. Don't leave me hanging here. Say something, or slap me across the face, or...something. Don't just stand there," Liam said desperately.

My emotions were so much on the surface tonight. I had been sobbing hysterically a few minutes ago, and now all I wanted to do was laugh. I began laughing and couldn't stop. I laughed so hard I started crying again. I stood on the porch of the house where my husband's mistress had lived, and I laughed. Liam watched me with a lost look on his face as I laughed at his declaration of love. I'm positive that was not the reaction he had been expecting.

I finally gained my composure, and saw the hurt on his face. Boy, had I blown it. Liam declared his love, and I had taken off into a giggling fit. Like a lightbulb going off in my brain, I realized I had let Jacob steal my joy for far too long.

Happiness was standing right in front of me and I was ready to reach out and grab it. The ghosts that lived in these houses couldn't haunt me anymore. I had exorcised them, right there in the driveway. I felt like a thousand pounds had been lifted off me. I knew for sure that what I felt was real. There was no denying it. I stood in front of Liam, put my arms around his neck, and pulled his face down to mine, kissing him tenderly. Pulling away, I looked directly into the eyes that had captured my heart from the beginning.

"Liam, I had no intention of falling in love with you. My life was perfectly fine the way it was. I swore when Jacob died no one was going to get close enough to hurt me again. I was great until you came along. I tried to avoid you. I tried to ignore you, but you wouldn't go away. Little by little, you broke down the walls until I had no choice but to let you in, and I am so glad that I did. Liam, I am so in love with you." I took a deep, shuddering breath as I finished.

"Now, that's a little more like it." He grabbed me and crushed my body against his. Our lips met in a heated kiss, right there on the front porch, and for once, I didn't care who saw.

He fumbled for his keys and managed to get the front door unlocked. We stumbled inside, wrapped around each other. My brain had turned to mush, but I did have one last coherent thought before I lost myself completely.

"I would love to see your bedroom," I said, giggling mischievously between kisses.

Liam let out a low groan, picked me up in his arms, and carried me upstairs.

Chapter Seventeen

Morning light filtered through the curtains. Feeling a bit disoriented, I shifted in the bed beside Liam. Looking around me, I tried to place my surroundings. It was that moment when you first wake up and you know you aren't in your own room, but can't quite remember where you are. Suddenly, the evening before came back to me in vivid detail. I recalled the drive to Liam's, the gut-punch when I realized where he lived, and the mutual declarations of love between us. I couldn't imagine an evening starting out as horribly as that one had. Somehow we navigated the crisis together, and it turned out better than I could have ever hoped.

I disentangled from Liam's arms and headed downstairs to his kitchen. I was starving, and I was sure he would be too when he awoke. It was only six in the morning, but my internal clock was set, making me a habitual early riser. I had to be on my way home within an hour to get the girls ready for school, so as much as I would have liked to lay there snuggled up with him, I knew I needed to get moving.

Looking in the refrigerator, two eggs and three slices of lunchmeat met my gaze. Liam hadn't left me much to work with. Thankfully, I found two slices of provolone as well. Cheese made everything better. I decided to whip up a small omelet for us to share. I cracked the two eggs into a bowl, found a whisk, and began mixing. I added salt and pepper, chopped the lunchmeat, gave it a final mix, and then poured it slowly into the sizzling pan.

Omelets were not my favorite thing to make, as they required patience, something I was sorely lacking. I always flipped the mixture too soon, making a mess of it in the process. Funny, I suddenly found myself comparing my love life to the omelet in front of me. I hoped I wasn't "flipping things" too soon with Liam. I sure didn't want to make a mess of that.

Deciding that it was now or never, I flipped the omelet in the pan, relieved that it was sheer perfection. It must be my lucky day. About that time, Liam wandered into the kitchen, wrapping his arms around me from behind. I certainly never got tired of this.

"Good morning," he said sleepily. "I woke up and you were gone. I didn't like it. Then I smelled something wonderful cooking down here and decided you were forgiven."

"Well, that's nice of you." I laughed. "There wasn't much in your refrigerator to work with. We get to split an omelet."

"Yeah, I haven't been here often enough to stock up on groceries. I seem to always be eating at your house these days, not that I'm complaining."

"I noticed that too, not that I'm complaining either," I responded, giving Liam a quick kiss as I handed him a plate of food.

He seated himself at the kitchen table, and I followed. I had found some coffee too, and poured us both a cup. He drank his coffee black. I, on the other hand, liked lots of cream and sugar in mine, both of which I thankfully found.

"So, no regrets about last night I hope?" Liam asked quietly. "I don't want to scare you. I do love you, but I don't want to rush you."

"You know, last night after I told you how I felt, I thought I might regret being so open. That was a huge step for me. You will be happy to know that after revisiting the conversation this morning while cooking your omelet, I wouldn't change a thing. I love you, too, and I'm not sorry I told you so." I looked into his eyes to be sure he knew how serious I was. This relationship was the best thing that had happened to me in a long time, and I was planning to do everything in my power to keep it.

I could see relief wash over Liam's face. I think he was convinced I would be spooked this morning after having time to think about things. That wasn't the case.

"So, I have to go out of town for a few days. I have some work in Chicago to check in on. I wouldn't go if I didn't have to, but my boss called yesterday and he needs me there to go over a case. Second pair of eyes, or something, to be sure he's not missing important details. I wish I didn't have to go." Liam looked at me uncertainly.

"I wish you didn't have to go too. I've become pretty used to seeing you every day. I don't think I'm going to like this at all. When do you leave?" I asked, unable to conceal my disappointment.

"I leave later this morning, actually. It's short notice, but that's the job. I'll be gone for four days. You know I'll call you pretty much a hundred times a day."

"You better. I think I'll miss the sound of your voice. I'm pretty sure I'll miss some other stuff too." I leaned in closely to kiss him.

We finished breakfast, and then cleaned up the kitchen. I felt a little wave of sadness inside. I was going to miss him. I realized just how inseparable we had become. I headed upstairs to get dressed. I needed to get the girls from Sadie and ready for school. Liam drove me home, and before I got out of the car I pulled him close to me, and gave him a long, lingering kiss.

"Hurry back," I said, holding him tightly for a moment.

"As fast as I can," Liam replied.

I grabbed my purse and opened the car door. Before I got out I turned to him and said, "I love you, Liam."

Smiling, Liam replied, "I love you too, Emma."

Deep inside, I knew that it was true.

Chapter Eighteen

I arrived home, looking at the clock on the wall and determining I had just enough time for a quick shower and change of clothes before going to get the girls. I let the steaming hot water wash over me. There was nothing like it to get me motivated in the morning. I turned off the water, dried myself off, and wrapped my hair in a towel. There wouldn't be time for fussing over my appearance today.

I grabbed a pair of jeans and a black blouse from the closet, quickly dressed, and then headed back into the bathroom. I removed the towel and set about combing my wavy hair. Today was a wash and wear kind of day if ever there was one. Luckily, my hair required little work. I put a quick shot of concealer under my eyes to cover the dark circles, applied two coats of mascara, some peach lip gloss, and was ready to go.

I was just heading out the front door to get the girls when the phone rang. I strode into the kitchen, picking up the phone on the third ring.

"Hello."

There was no answer. This was exactly what had happened the day of the backyard barbeque. I was beginning to get irritated.

"Hello," I repeated. "Is someone there?"

"I know you know where they are," a deep, menacing male voice said.

"I'm sorry." Confusion filled me. "I think you have the wrong number."

"I know you know where they are, and you better tell me. If you don't, you're going to be sorry," he said again.

Before I could respond, the line went dead. He had hung up. That was very strange. I felt certain it had been a wrong number. I definitely didn't recognize the voice. He was so intimidating, though, I felt a bit shaken.

"I know you know where they are," I repeated aloud. I racked my brain to think of who it could be and what he could be talking about. Coming up with no good answers, I decided it must have been a wrong number. The caller had such a menacing voice. Just the sound of it gave me chills. I grabbed my purse and headed out the front door, pushing thoughts of the random phone call out of my mind.

After putting the girls on the bus, I went next door to Morning Glory. The place was already busy, and there wasn't an open table. Jane had things running smoothly, as usual, but I jumped right in to help. We worked together systematically during the morning rush. We were such a great team we didn't even require words. Once things slowed down, Jane and I had a break before we needed to get ready for the lunch rush.

"So, how are things with you and Liam?" Jane asked as she wiped down tables.

"They're great. He is amazing in so many ways. The girls love him. I love him…I mean, literally. I told him I loved him. Can you believe that? But, I keep finding myself waiting for the other shoe to drop. I don't know why I can't just relax."

"Jacob hurt you, that's why," Jane replied in her no-nonsense way. "That jerk never deserved you, and when he betrayed you, I watched you hide inside yourself. You've stayed there all these years. I am glad Liam has been able to draw you out. Don't fight that, girl. He's a good man."

"Yes, he is a wonderful man. I guess I'm just having a hard time accepting that good things can happen to me."

I wasn't sure why I couldn't shake the feeling of doom. I thought back to this morning, and the look on Liam's face as he kissed me goodbye. The man really did love me. I believed that with all of my heart. I just needed to remember that, and push all of the negative thoughts aside.

Jane and I finished out the afternoon working side by side. I was filling the sugar containers on the tables before I finished up for the day. We had been so busy that it seemed as if they were all empty. It felt good to be productive. Glancing at the clock, I realized the girls were due home in a few minutes. I told Jane goodbye, leaving the closing of the shop to her.

I ran into the house to start a load of laundry as soon as the girls came home. Sometimes my afternoons felt like the movie Groundhog Day. The order sometimes varied, but the duties were always the same; rush upstairs, grab the always full hamper, carry it downstairs to the laundry room, put a load in, meet the bus, watch the girls race toward me on the porch and be bombarded as all three vied for my attention, all talking at once, and then head inside to help with homework and start dinner. Often, the sheer rush of it sent my head spinning, but staying on top of things was the only way I could handle it all. It was a carefully choreographed dance, each step important in its own way.

"Mama, I have a reading contest at school this month. Mrs. Vickers said whoever reads the most books wins a prize. I'm going to win," Dahlia said excitedly.

"With the way you read, it won't surprise me at all." I kissed my baby on the top of the head. I was a proud mama. "Why don't you get out the new book I bought for you and get started?"

"Okay, Mama," Dahlia ran upstairs to get started.

Tacos sounded good for dinner, so I got out the vegetables and began chopping. Lily and Rose were busy doing homework, and Dahlia was working on her reading project. The house was strangely quiet for the middle of the afternoon.

I realized I really missed Liam. I didn't like the quiet. Since Liam had been in my life, the quiet had subsided. He was usually with us at this time of day, and his absence was noticeable. That may be why I jumped when my phone rang. Looking at the number coming across my cellphone screen, I smiled upon seeing Liam's number.

"Hello." Just the thought of him made me happy. "I was just thinking about you."

"Hey, honey. How are you doing? What are you making for dinner? Did the girls get home from school okay?" Liam asked each question in succession.

I smiled to myself as I realized he knew our afternoon routine so well that he was aware exactly what we'd all be doing at this very minute. I had become so used to him being around that it left a huge hole in the house when he was gone.

"Yes, the girls are here. They're working on homework. Dahlia is busy reading so she can win the class reading prize. I'm making tacos for dinner," I continued to fill Liam in on the details as I prepared dinner. "You made it to Chicago okay?"

"Yep, I landed a few hours ago. I've already been to the office. The boss filled me in on the case. I don't think it will take that long here. I may even be home sooner than I thought." I could almost hear the smile in his voice. "I can't believe how much I miss you already."

"Me, too. I was just thinking how quiet it is here without you. I don't like it one bit." I laughed.

We talked for several more minutes. I didn't want to hang up. I wanted to keep that connection, even if it was only by phone. I was severely hooked on this man. He hadn't even been gone a full day yet and I was having withdrawal. Being around Liam was like a drug for me. It made me feel good to know that he felt the same way. Reluctantly, we said goodbye to each other, with Liam promising to call tomorrow morning. That seemed like a lifetime away. I was in sad shape. I hung up the phone and called the girls down to dinner.

The tacos were a huge success, and the girls ate so much I didn't even have anything to box up for leftovers, which made me happy.

I sent Lily and Dahlia upstairs to get showers while I finished cleaning up the kitchen. I told them to hurry so that I could help Rose with her bath when they were done.

After tucking the girls into bed and putting the last load of laundry in the dryer for the night, I headed to my room to unwind before going to sleep. I climbed into bed, turned on the TV and settled myself into a comfortable position. I had become so accustomed to sharing my nights with Liam that the bed felt strangely empty. It was going to be a very long four days.

I watched some mindless reality television for a bit and realized I was getting tired. I was about to turn it off and go to sleep when the phone rang. The number on my cellphone came up "Unavailable." Normally, I wouldn't answer a number I didn't recognize, but I thought maybe Liam was calling from a different number. I decided to answer.

"Hello."

There was no answer, but a very distinct sound of someone breathing on the other end. This was exactly the same thing that had happened twice already. This time, though, he'd called my cellphone. I didn't give that number out to everyone, so who was this?

"Hello," I said, beginning to feel uneasy as it slowly dawned on me that a stranger had somehow gotten my cellphone number.

"Hello, Emma." It was the same chilling, menacing male voice. As soon as I heard it, my stomach knotted up and my pulse quickened. I racked my brain trying to figure out why this person kept calling me. What could he possibly want from me? I was just a normal woman, and to the best of my knowledge, I had no enemies. I certainly didn't have anything to hide. He had said "I know you

101

know where they are" when he last called me. What did I have? I was confused, but I was also beginning to be very frightened. This person obviously thought I had something he wanted. But what?

"Who is this?" I demanded.

"You don't recognize me, Emma? We spoke this morning. I told you that you had better tell me what you know. Do you believe that I'm serious now?" he continued.

"I don't know what you're talking about. What is it I supposedly know that I'm not telling you?" I tried hard to control the fear in my voice. Panic had fully set in, and I realized that I potentially had a very real problem on my hands. I had no idea what he wanted, but he was definitely not giving up. He seemed to know my name, know me, and that terrified me beyond belief.

"I want to know where they are. You're going to tell me, or else you will not enjoy the consequences."

"I don't know what you mean."

"Perhaps you should ask your boyfriend," he said. "Don't worry, I'll be in touch." He hung up the phone.

I sat on my bed, not sure what to do. There was no denying that it wasn't a wrong number. The stranger had said my name. He knew who I was. Suddenly, I was very afraid. If he had my number that also meant he knew where I lived. Was I in some kind of danger? I got up and looked out my bedroom window at the dark street below. I didn't see anyone, but definitely had the feeling of being watched. Maybe he was out there, sitting in the shadows watching me. For the first time in years I was afraid inside my own house.

I paced, not sure what to do next. Should I call the police? What would I tell them if I called? There didn't really seem to be anything they could do. The man hadn't done anything, other than call. I'm sure it wasn't a police matter. I considered calling Sadie, but then remembered she left town this afternoon to visit her mom. Should I call

Liam? He was in Chicago, and I didn't want to worry him. Knowing Liam and his fiercely protective nature, he would race back here immediately if he even suspected I might be in danger. I couldn't have him putting his job in jeopardy because I was afraid. He was in Chicago because he was needed on a case. I couldn't interfere with that just because of a phone call. I was just going to handle this myself. I was an adult. I was competent. I could take care of myself. I went downstairs to check the doors and windows. Everything was locked up tight, but I was still afraid.

I returned to my room and crawled into bed. For the first time since I was a young child, I decided to sleep with the light on. I was on edge, though, and sleep eluded me for a very long time. When it finally did come, it was a fitful, restless sleep.

I dreamed I was alone in the forest. It was dark and cold, and I was being pursued by a stranger. I couldn't see his face, but I could hear his voice. He called my name as he ran after me. I could hear him coming closer and closer. He chased me through the trees. I was in my nightgown, barefoot, frantically running as fast as I could. I knew that I couldn't run fast enough to outrun him. My lungs felt like they were on fire. I could tell he was gaining on me. I realized I was literally running for my life. My nightgown caught on a tree branch, and ripped in half. I tried to grab it to cover myself, which caused me to lose my footing. I stumbled, falling onto the forest floor. The man closed in on me. He reached down and grabbed my wrist. Panic seized me as I let out a scream. I knew it was too late. I couldn't get away from him.

I sat up in bed, awakening from the dream. Sunlight filtered in through the windows, and I realized it was morning.

Chapter Twenty

I got out of bed, exhausted. I could already tell that this was going to be a bad day. I had barely slept, and what I had gotten was definitely not restful. It had been interrupted by dreams of the stranger and his stupid phone calls. On top of being bone-weary, I was still spooked from last night, and worried someone was stalking me. Things like this didn't happen to ordinary people like me. This was something that happened to other people.

The thought that had me the most concerned was how the stranger had gotten my phone number. It was terrifying to me that he knew my name. What else did he know about me? Had he been following the girls and me? Had he been to the house? A million questions ran through my head, causing the uneasy feeling to take up residence. I felt as if I had been violated and made to feel unsafe in my own home. It made me angry.

I debated again whether or not to tell Liam. Part of me wanted to, and to have him race home and protect me like I knew he would. Another part of me, the part that I had relied on for many years, told me that I was completely capable of taking care of myself and I didn't need to be rescued. Old habits die hard, and that was the side that won out in the end. Chances are the stalker probably wouldn't call me again, so there was no need to make a big deal of it. Convincing myself that this was true, I set about getting ready for the grueling day ahead. I tried my best to put the events of last night out of my mind in the hopes that it would not be a recurring event. I tried to convince myself that things were not as bad as they had seemed.

I was at Morning Glory brewing a fresh cup of coffee for a customer when I got the distinct feeling I was being watched. I looked out the large windows along the front of my shop. Everything looked normal. I needed to get a firm grasp on myself before I completely lost touch with reality. Yet, my gut instinct kept screaming I was being watched.

I was about to go back to work when I spotted the same car I saw the day I had walked to Trés Chic. I remembered I had felt uneasy and a sense I was being followed. The man I saw, all dressed in black was now leaning on his car across the street from my shop. He was again wearing black, with black sunglasses and a black ball cap. I couldn't have identified any of his facial features if I wanted to, and I had the sudden thought that he probably wanted it that way.

Was I being paranoid? I didn't think so. This was a small town, and I recognized most people in it. I didn't recognize this man, and I had seen him twice now. Both times left me uneasy. I had learned a long time ago to trust my intuition, and that's what I did now.

Deciding I was going to find out once and for all who he was and what he wanted, I walked out the front door of the coffee shop and headed right in his direction. He saw me coming, pulled his ball cap down lower, got into his car, and quickly started the ignition. Before I could get to him, he pulled out of the parking space, tires screeching as he sped away.

Now I was sure this man was up to no good, and that he was definitely targeting me. My gut told me he was the one who had made the phone calls. The problem was I had no idea what to do with the information. I hadn't reacted quickly enough to get his license plate number, and I was back to square one.

Frustrated, I headed back inside Morning Glory. Jane looked at me questioningly, probably wondering what had possessed me to walk out like that. I wasn't in the mood to answer questions, so I headed to the back to work in my office.

About now I was questioning my judgement in not telling Liam about the man and the phone calls, but I wasn't second-guessing the fact that I didn't want him to see me as a helpless woman. I had taken care of myself for years before he came along. I was certain I could still. If things got worse, I would tell Liam at that point. I was just going to be extra cautious for the next few days, and be sure I was aware of my surroundings at all times.

I worked for the next hour or so on projects at my desk. My traumatic night finally caught up with me, though, and I developed a pounding headache. Deciding to go home and lie down for a bit, I headed up front to tell Jane. She looked concerned, but readily agreed, telling me she had it under control and not to worry. As I bee-lined toward the door, her question, "is everything all right," reached my ears. I knew my behavior was out of the ordinary, and I probably should have told her what was going on. I just didn't want to put a voice to my concerns yet. "Everything's fine," I lied, "Just didn't sleep well with Liam out of town." I gave a weak laugh and wave and abruptly retreated home.

Unlocking the front door, the quiet greeted me. My head felt like it was going to explode, and I needed sleep. I had two hours before the girls were home from school. Making sure I locked the front door securely behind me, I headed upstairs to my room. I went to the medicine cabinet, opened it, found the pain reliever, popped two Ibuprofen in my mouth, washed them down with some water, and crawled into my still unmade bed. I lay down, letting the quietness settle around me. Normally, I would be happy for an afternoon nap in a peaceful house, but after last night and this afternoon, I was tense at the thought of being alone. Knowing I had to sleep if I had any hope of functioning once the girls got home, I closed my eyes, willing the Ibuprofen to kick in.

I drifted off fairly quickly, but nightmares overtook my mind. I dreamed I was again running, being pursued by an unknown man. I couldn't see his face, but I could hear his breath coming fast and hard behind me as he chased me down a darkened alley. I ran as fast as my legs would carry me, but still I could feel him gaining on me. I panted, breathing hard, as he pursued me ruthlessly. I could feel him close behind me. Suddenly, he reached out and grabbed my hair, causing me to tumble onto the pavement below me. I tried to scream, but no sound came out. I knew there was no escape for me now. His face was shadowed by the night, and I had no idea who he was, but he seemed to know me. "Hello, Emma. We finally meet," he said, in a voice that made my blood run cold.

The alarm on my phone went off, thankfully tearing me out of the frightening dream. I fumbled to turn off the alarm, grateful for the interruption of the terror in my mind. If I continued to be plagued with dreams every time I slept, I knew that it wouldn't be long before the stress of it all took its toll on me.

Mercifully, at least my headache was gone. I definitely did not feel rested, though. It didn't matter, because it was time for the girls to be getting off of the bus. I headed downstairs and walked outside just as the bus rounded the corner. Lying on my front porch was a bouquet of dead roses.

Chapter Twenty-One

I reached down and grabbed the dead flowers in my shaking hands. This was definitely not a coincidence. Whoever this man was, he was trying to scare me. I had to admit he was doing a spectacular job of it. I tossed the dead flowers into the trash can at the end of the driveway, plastered a fake smile on my face, took a deep breath, and went to the curb to get my children off of the bus.

The girls were in good moods, which I was grateful for. I needed something to get my mind off of what was going on. I tried hard not to let the girls know anything was wrong. The last thing I wanted was for them to feel unsafe. Their safety and well-being were my only concerns, and I would not have it taken away by some stalker with a vendetta.

We went inside and began our usual afternoon ritual of homework. I didn't want to cook, so I called in an order for pizza, which made the girls happy. With dinner out of the way, I went over my mental to-do list. Normally, my daily chores were a burden, but today I was grateful for the sense of normalcy they lent. I was heading to the laundry room to put in an obligatory load when my cellphone rang. I cringed at the sound, praying that it wasn't the stranger again. I didn't think I could handle any more drama right now.

I grabbed my phone off the counter, ready to give this man a piece of my mind. Looking at the display, I saw with relief it was Liam.

"Hey, there." I tried to sound lighthearted. "How are you doing?"

"Not as good as if I were home with my girls. But, seriously, things here are progressing pretty well. I have some good news for you." Liam's voice was a soothing balm to my frazzled nerves.

"What's the news?" I was grateful for anything to

distract me from my current situation.

"I'll be home tomorrow. I can't wait to see you."

"Oh, Liam, I am so glad you're coming home early." Unable to contain the relief in my voice, I nearly burst into tears. I warned myself to keep it together.

"Honey, is everything okay? You don't sound like yourself."

"I'm fine," I lied. "I just miss you. I'm really glad it didn't take as long as you thought it would."

"Me, too. I had no idea how much I would miss you and the girls. My manliness has been compromised. Apparently, I'm totally under your spell, seeing as I can't even make it two days away from you without turning into a pile of mush." Liam laughed on the other end of the phone.

"Well, I don't mind a little mush every now and then. I'll be really happy to see you." I meant it with everything in me.

We talked a little more, and then the girls wanted to speak to him as well. It was cute to hear them on the phone with him, knowing they missed him as much as I did. We said goodbye to each other, and I hung up, grateful I only had one more day until he would be back in Beckland.

Later that night, the girls were tucked into bed and the last load of laundry was almost done drying. I had a few things to do downstairs, and I needed to clean up the kitchen. I was almost finished loading the dishwasher when I heard my phone chime, alerting me I had a new text message. Smiling, I thought it was probably Liam texting me to say goodnight. He was so sweet. I grabbed the phone and clicked on the message icon.

My heart began to pound. It came from an unavailable number. With trepidation, I opened the message and saw it was a picture taken the day we had the backyard barbecue. Under the photo was the text that simply read, "I see you."

The photo was taken from an angle which made it clear that the photographer was taking the picture through the slats of a fence. Looking more closely, I realized it was the fence in my backyard. Someone had taken a picture of Sadie, Liam, the girls, and me when we were eating dinner. Whoever it was had been watching us while we were totally unaware. I felt like I had been violated in so many ways. I was also terrified, knowing that the stalker had been that close to me and my family and I had been completely oblivious.

Angrily, I deleted the message, just wanting it to go away. I was livid this man had tainted my memory of that special day with my family. How dare he? Then I realized that deleting the photo was probably a mistake. Maybe the number could have been traced. I might need that picture for evidence. How could I have been so stupid as to delete it?

At that moment, I knew with certainty I had to tell Liam about this as soon as he came home. There was no more denying and pretending I could handle this on my own. I couldn't. This was way bigger than I had thought. Seeing the picture and knowing the man had practically been in my backyard let me know I couldn't deal with this without help. The girls and I were in very real danger.

I finished cleaning up the kitchen and decided to call it a night, although with my nerves on high alert I knew sleep would be a long time coming. I checked the doors and windows throughout the house twice, making sure that they were locked tight. I hated feeling so unsafe. A complete stranger had managed to rob me of my feelings of security.

Satisfied the house was locked up, I headed upstairs. As I expected, I was too worked up to sleep, and just laid there in bed, unable to stop my mind from racing. I tried to decide how I was going to tell Liam. It was very important to me not to come across as needy, but maybe my pride didn't even matter anymore. I did need Liam.

Maybe he wouldn't see it as a sign of weakness. My pride was inconsequential if it stood in the way of my family's safety. I would be negligent to stick my head in the sand and pretend everything was fine. I would tell Liam tomorrow, as soon as he was home. With that knowledge in my mind, I turned off the lights and tried my best to get some sleep.

Chapter Twenty-Two

Once again, my night was filled with horrible, terrifying dreams. I hadn't slept well in several days, and I could feel it catching up to me. I was tired and especially grouchy as I woke the girls up for school. For their sakes, I hoped they would cooperate with me this morning. I didn't like losing my temper with them, and I was afraid I would if they gave me problems getting ready for school today.

Thankfully, they must have gauged my mood and decided it wasn't a great day to mess with Mom. I had a terrible poker face, and I didn't cover my bad mood well. "Mama, are you okay?" Rose asked as I put scrambled eggs onto their plates.

"Yeah, honey, I'm okay," I said, trying to sound lighthearted. "I just didn't sleep well last night and I'm kind of tired today."

"You should take a nap, Mom," Dahlia said, sounding concerned.

"Yeah, Mom, why don't you stay home today and get some rest? You know Jane will run the shop," added Lily.

"You girls are sweet to be concerned for me. I'm going to be fine. Don't you worry," I said, throwing in a smile to be convincing. I told myself to pull it together. It wasn't my daughters' job to be worried about me.

I didn't want to tell them that the last thing I wanted today was to be home by myself. I was afraid to be in my own home. That was a horrible feeling, and it frustrated me that a stranger had made me feel that way. Angry, scared, emotional Emma was not a good combination.

I think I deserved an Academy Award for my performance during the remainder of breakfast. I convinced the girls that Mom was going to be all right, and they kissed me goodbye and headed to the bus. I finished cleaning up the kitchen quickly and dragged myself next door to work, making sure the door was locked behind me.

I settled into my office at Morning Glory while the breakfast rush was underway up front. I didn't have it in me to deal with customers this morning. Jane had it well under control, so I was able to get caught up on paperwork. I was just going through my invoices when I heard someone come in. I assumed it was Jane, needing to ask me a question, so I didn't even look up.

"That's not a very good welcome home," I heard Liam say from the doorway.

I popped my head up. I had never been so glad to see someone in my life. Suddenly everything was okay. I was safe. The girls were safe. A part of me hated that I needed him near me to feel safe, but I couldn't deny that it was the case. I was just thankful that he was home. I jumped up from my desk and ran across the room to him. I flung myself into his arms, hanging on for dear life. I never wanted to be away from him again.

"Well, that's more like it." He laughed, running his fingers through my hair.

"I missed you so much. I'm so glad you're back. Please tell me you don't have to go again anytime soon," I said, realizing how desperate I sounded, but not caring.

"Hey, wait a minute. What's wrong? This is more than missing me," Liam said, seeing right through me. "Sit down and tell me what's going on."

Liam knew me well. I was absolutely transparent to him. The time for stalling was over. The time had come to tell him, so I sat back down at my desk and directed him to one of the office chairs across from me. He looked at me curiously, uncertain of what was going on.

"Well, there is something…something I haven't told you. First of all, you have to promise not to be mad at me for not telling you sooner. It's just that counting on someone to help me is new territory. It doesn't come naturally, and my first instinct is to take care of the problem myself, so that's what I did," I began, wanting to lay the groundwork for what I was about to say.

"Emma, I will not be mad at you. Just tell me what's going on, please." Liam looked at me with such worry.

"Okay, do you remember when we had the barbecue in the back yard? Remember that weird phone call I got? The one where I could hear the person breathing, but no one answered?"

"Yeah, I remember. What about it?"

"Well, I got a couple more of those phone calls over the next few days. Always someone there, I could hear them breathing, but no one ever answered. I just ignored them, thinking it was a wrong number." I continued feeling nervous recounting the story.

"Go on," Liam encouraged, looking uneasy.

"The first night you were in Chicago, I got another phone call. By this time, I was irritated because I knew someone was on the line. This call was different, though, because the person on the phone used my name. He said he knew that I knew where "they" were and that I had better tell him. He also said that my boyfriend knew more than he was telling me." I swallowed hard, getting up from my chair and pacing the floor as I relived the story.

"Then, the next day at work I saw a man watching me through the windows. I had seen him before. The day I walked to town right after you and I met. He had made me uneasy that day, he was just parking his car, for heaven's sake, but I ignored it. It was the same guy, watching me. I went outside the shop and walked toward him. I was going to confront him…"

"Confront him?" Liam shot up from the chair. "Emma, are you out of your mind? What were you thinking?" Liam interrupted, running his hands through his hair as he did when he was frustrated.

"You promised not to get mad, Liam. Just please let

me get through this without interrupting me,"

"Sorry. Go on." Liam resumed his seat, and looked more than a little frustrated with me.

"Anyway, when he saw me coming, he jumped in his car and sped away. I didn't get his license plate number, and I'm awful with the make and model of cars, so don't even ask me. Later that night, I got a text message. The number was unavailable, but when I opened it, it was a picture of us on the day of the barbecue. It read, "I see you." Liam, I don't know what this is about, but I'm telling you because I'm afraid. I have been having nightmares, and I haven't slept in days. I'm frightened to be home alone, and when I am there, I'm constantly checking the doors and windows to be sure they're locked. I'm going a little crazy, and I don't know what to do now," I finished, glad to finally have it off of my chest. I was getting teary-eyed, and I tried hard to hold it in.

Liam sat there for a few minutes, not saying a word, not looking at me, but staring past me. I couldn't tell if he was mad at me or not.

"Would you please say something? You're making me nervous."

"First of all, I am not mad at you. I'm frustrated with you for keeping secrets from me. I get it, though. You're not used to having someone there to help you, and I'm trying to keep that in mind as I try not to be frustrated with you."

"Look, I'm sorry. If I could go back again, I would have told you the first time I started to get nervous. But I'm telling you now. I don't know what to do about this. I need your help."

"Okay, well, we are definitely taking this seriously. Fortunately, this is right up my alley, and I know how to protect you and the girls. From here on out, I don't want you to be alone at all. I'm moving my things into your house today. I'm going to stay there until we figure out who this creep is and what he wants," Liam said with authority.

Whatever my misgivings might have been about him staying with the girls and me, I pushed them aside when I saw his jaw was set with determination. The only thing that mattered right now was the safety of the girls, and I was willing to do whatever I needed to in order to make that happen. If that meant that Liam stayed at our house, then I was fine with that.

"Okay. I'm not going to argue with you. I don't want the girls to be afraid though, so we need to come up with a good reason for you moving in. We'll tell them that your house is being painted or something and that you need a place to stay." I formulated a plan in my head as I spoke.

"That's fine. Tell the girls whatever you need to, but I will be staying there. I will not let anything happen to you or to them. I promise." Liam reached across the desk to grab my hands. "I will find out who this guy is, you can be sure of that."

My heart practically leaped out of my chest with love for Liam. His fiercely protective nature was one of the things I admired most about him. The knots that had been in my stomach for the past several days began to slowly untwist. Tension left my shoulders, and I was sure Liam would do everything in his power to keep us secure.

"You finish working. I'm going over to my place to grab the things I'll need. What time are you done here? I'll be sure that I'm back to walk you home."

"Walk me home? Liam, it's ten feet from here to the house. I think I can manage." I rolled my eyes, thinking he was overreacting.

"Emma, when I say that I don't want you alone, I mean I don't want you alone at all. Not for even a second," Liam replied. "We are not arguing this point."

"Okay. I'll be finishing up here around three-thirty. That's when the girls get home from school," I said, deciding it was best not to argue with him in his current state.

"I'll be back before three-thirty. Do not leave until I get here." Liam bent down to kiss me goodbye quickly before he headed out the door.

If I hadn't been so afraid of the stranger, I might have been irritated at the degree of overprotectiveness from Liam. Were we both blowing this entire thing out of proportion? I knew Liam's detective instincts were out in full force, and I had to admit that made me feel safe. I decided to go along and do things his way, erring on the side of caution.

***

Liam drove his Mustang toward home, making a mental checklist of things he needed to take to Emma's. He was stumped on who could be stalking her. Few things took him by surprise, but this had. He berated himself for not noticing sooner that something was wrong. He was an FBI agent, for crying out loud! It was his job to be hyper-vigilant and always aware. This had definitely snuck up on him, though. He was having a hard time thinking rationally, since it had to do with Emma's safety. Taking a few deep breaths, he forced himself into detective mode.

He needed to separate his feelings for Emma from the facts. In the case of a stalker, it was almost always someone the victim knew. Most stalkers were angry ex-husbands or ex-boyfriends, but Emma didn't have either. Oftentimes it was someone the victim had wronged in some way. In the time he had known Emma, he hadn't come across a single person that had a bad thing to say about her. She was beloved by everyone who knew her. He couldn't imagine her having any enemies. The only concrete facts were a few phone calls, a text message, a couple of sightings, and some dead roses. That really wasn't a lot to go on.

All at once, the back of Liam's neck began to tingle.

The hairs on his arms stood up. His physical responses let him know that his detective instincts were finally kicking in. These things always happened to him when a case began coming together in his head, and he knew he was on the right track. He needed to look at this from a different angle. Maybe it wasn't an enemy of Emma's at all. What if the person was somehow connected to him? Yes, he felt sure he was on the right path now. He could feel the puzzle pieces swirling around in his mind, trying to form a complete picture. It was still elusive, and he definitely needed to think about it more. His stomach knotted at the thought that he may have inadvertently put the woman he loved in danger. He would not leave her side until he figured this out.

Chapter Twenty-Three

True to his word, Liam arrived back at Morning Glory by three p.m. He came into the shop and asked me for my house key so he could unload his car. I made a mental note to get him a copy made if he was going to be there for a while. A few weeks ago the thought of Liam moving into my house would have sent me into a full-blown panic attack. Living in the same house was going to seriously change our relationship. I was hoping it would change it in a good way. With all that had happened, though, I was just grateful that he was there. I gave him the key and he headed out the door, telling me he would be back in thirty minutes and not to step outside until he arrived.

"Quite possessive, isn't he?" Jane observed, unaware of the reason for Liam's protectiveness.

"No, he really isn't. There are some things going on that I haven't told you, Jane. I don't want to go into it again, but take my word Liam is just doing what is necessary right now." I wished I had it in me to share my problems with Jane.

"Well, I won't pry into your business, sweetheart, but you know you can tell me anything." Jane patted my shoulder, reassuringly.

"And I will tell you. Soon. I just can't talk about it right now." I forced myself to smile at Jane, even though I didn't feel like it.

Thirty minutes later, Liam appeared in the front door of Morning Glory. I told Jane I was heading home, and she gave me a concerned smile. I knew she was worried about what was going on.

Not for the first time in the last couple of days, I wished Sadie were here. She was visiting her mom in New York. She had only been gone a few days, but I already missed her dreadfully. Not wanting to ruin her vacation, I hadn't even called her to tell her what was going on.

Liam walked home with me and we arrived as the bus did. The girls ran to greet him as soon as they saw that he was with me. I hadn't told them he was coming home early, so they were surprised. They had missed him too. I could tell from the huge smile on Liam's face that the feeling was mutual. Our living situation would be a real test of our relationship, and one that I prayed it could withstand.

"It's so good to see you girls," Liam said, pulling them all to him in a big hug. "I sure did miss you."

"We missed you too," Rose answered, planting a kiss on Liam's cheek.

"Not as much as mom did, though. She has been moping around the house for days," Lily said, glancing my way.

"I have not been moping," I said, looking at Liam. Liam just looked back at me, a worried expression fixed on his face.

"Who has homework that I can help with?" Liam asked the girls, in an effort to change the subject.

"You can help me," Dahlia replied. "I have a spelling test tomorrow. You can ask me the words and I will spell them for you."

"Perfect," Liam said. "Spelling is my favorite."

Liam and Dahlia settled themselves in the living room for a spelling quiz and Rose and Lily headed for the kitchen. I joined them to figure out what to make for dinner. I was deep in thought, trying to figure out how to explain the new living situation to the girls. I didn't want them to get used to Liam being here when I knew it wasn't a permanent situation, but I also knew the girls and I needed his protection. I was trying to figure out how to go about it so it didn't seem like a big deal.

"Is Liam staying for dinner, Mom?" Lily asked, looking up from her Social Studies homework.

I decided that was the lead-in I needed, so I called

everyone into the kitchen. Once they were settled, I dove in with the news.

"Yes, Lily, Liam is staying for dinner. In fact, Liam will be staying with us for a while. He's having some painting done on his new house, and he needs a place to stay," I began, lying smoothly. "We don't want him inhaling fresh paint fumes, do we? I told him that he could stay here with us, and I didn't think you girls would mind."

"We don't mind mom," Dahlia said excitedly.

"Yeah, that will be kind of cool," Lily agreed.

"Where is Liam going to sleep?" Rose asked, taking me by surprise. Leave it to Rose to ask the one question I didn't want to answer.

"Well, Rose, Liam is going to sleep in the uh…maybe in…" I stuttered, not sure how to answer this question without inviting an entirely different discussion than I was ready to have with my daughters.

"On the couch…" Liam finished for me. "I'm going to sleep on the couch. I've slept on a lot of couches in my day." He shot me a grin.

I looked at him gratefully, happy that he rescued me. I did not want to have a conversation on adult sleeping arrangements with my children.

"Yes, Liam will be sleeping on the couch."

"I appreciate you girls letting me hang out here while they work on my house. I think it might be fun for all of us. I have a great idea. Why don't you girls help me fix dinner tonight while Mom goes upstairs and takes a nice, long, hot bath? She is looking kind of tired."

"Yeah, Mama, go take a hot bath," Lily agreed. "We will fix you dinner tonight."

"Well, I guess I could do that. If you're sure…" I trailed off, not used to this kind of thing. This was definitely not the way a normal afternoon played out for me.

"Of course I'm sure. If I'm going to stay here, I'm

going to help you out. Don't worry, I won't burn anything," Liam said, giving me a teasing smile.

After being assured and reassured he and the girls had everything under control, I headed upstairs for my bath. This was a luxury I was not accustomed to. It might not be so bad to have Liam here after all. Not that I had anticipated it being bad...I just thought it would be awkward, and send me into a bit of a panic. Surprisingly, though, I felt nothing but relief and gratefulness.

I headed into my bathroom and turned on the hot water. I put some bubble bath into the tub, and let the water fill pretty much to capacity. After turning the faucet off, I stepped in and slid my body down into the water. It felt so good to not be worried for a few minutes. I had been on edge for days. As I slid further into the tub, I felt the tension ease a little.

I knew that I could de-stress with Liam in charge. I laid my head against the back of the tub and closed my eyes. The hot water began to reduce my tense muscles. I tried to clear my mind and fully give in to the relaxation I desperately needed. The sleeplessness of the last few days began to catch up to me, and I realized that I was exhausted. I closed my eyes and slowly drifted off to sleep.

When I awakened, it wasn't to a tub full of cold water. I opened my eyes, trying to orient myself to my surroundings. I was lying in my bed, wrapped in a large, fluffy bath towel, covered by the plush blanket that I kept at the bottom of the bed. I looked at my bedside clock, which said it was nine p.m. What was going on? It had been four in the afternoon when I had come upstairs to take a bath. I remembered running the water and sliding inside. I remembered how relaxed I had been. I also vaguely remembered falling asleep. What I didn't remember was getting out of the tub and getting into my bed. Had I been sleepwalking? What had happened to the last five hours?

I headed to my bathroom, grabbed my robe, and

headed down the hall, fully expecting chaos. I was sure that the girls were running around, playing, not ready for bed. What disaster had they made while I had been asleep? Had they even eaten dinner? I shook my head as I imagined the mess I was about to encounter in my kitchen.

As I passed the girls' rooms, though, I couldn't believe what I was seeing. There they were, sound asleep. They were clean, in pajamas, and expertly tucked into bed. I continued downstairs. I headed to the kitchen, where I was met with an immaculately cleaned room. Dishes were done, counters were cleaned, and I noticed coffee was even made and the timer was already set for tomorrow. From the kitchen, I could see Liam, seated on the couch in the living room, watching a basketball game. What was going on here? Had I entered some alternate universe?

I walked into the living room, and Liam noticed me for the first time.

"Hey, sleepyhead." He grinned at me.

"Hey." I plopped down on the couch next to him. I could not figure out what was going on. "Maybe you can tell me where the last five hours of my life went?"

"Well, you went upstairs to take a bath, and the girls and I fixed some chicken Alfredo. They were a lot of help, actually. They like to cook. I think they were a little surprised that I knew what I was doing. After that, we finished homework. They only argued with me a little bit. Then, I sent them up to take their baths, I read them all a story, and tucked them into bed. Then I cleaned up the kitchen and decided to watch some basketball," Liam answered matter-of-factly. "Oh, yeah, I kept a plate of dinner warming for you in the oven."

Liam went to the kitchen and returned with a plate of chicken Alfredo, warmed to the perfect temperature. He also brought me a fork and a napkin, and set it all on a TV tray in front of me. I just looked at him, not really sure what to say. He really was too good to be true. I suddenly realized how hungry I was, and began eating. The food was delicious. Was there anything he couldn't do?

"You did all of that while I was asleep? I must have been out of it. I don't even remember getting out of the bathtub," I replied, more confused than I had been.

"You didn't actually get out of the bathtub. After the girls and I had dinner ready for you, I came upstairs to let you know. You were sound asleep. Your water was ice cold. I couldn't believe you could sleep through that, and I was worried you were going to drown. So, I grabbed a bath towel and wrapped you up in it. I carried you to bed and laid you down. I was going to dress you, but I was sure that would wake you up, and I really just wanted you to sleep. I covered you up with your blanket so you wouldn't get cold, and came back downstairs with the girls. We ate and finished up all of the chores for the night, and then they went to bed. Pretty simple, really. Oh, yeah, and I folded the load of laundry you had in the dryer and started another load."

I couldn't believe what I was hearing. What Liam had done was anything but simple. I know because I did all of those things every day. If I hadn't already been head over heels for him, this would definitely have been my tipping point.

"You're amazing. I don't even really have words right now. I'm just so glad you're here," I said, my eyes filling with tears.

"Does this mean that I don't have to sleep on the couch tonight?" A mischievous look danced in his eyes.

"You most definitely don't have to sleep on the couch tonight." I took his hand and led him up the stairs toward my bedroom.

Chapter Twenty-Four

I slept better than I had in days. I thought I would have trouble falling asleep after my five hour nap, but I was apparently so sleep-deprived that it wasn't a problem for me. When I woke the next morning, Liam was gone. I wondered where he was. I grabbed my robe and put it on, heading downstairs. I found him on the couch, sound asleep. I hadn't even heard him leave the bed, and had no idea how long he had been down here. I assumed he wanted the girls to think he had slept down here the entire night. He was so sweet and considerate of their feelings. He was a good man. I definitely hit the jackpot with him.

I went into the kitchen to start breakfast, deciding to stick with simple toast and scrambled eggs today. I was trying to move quietly, so as not to wake him. I poured a cup of coffee to get me going. I found the ingredients, and then went upstairs to wake the girls. Unbelievably, they got out of bed with only the minimal amount of grumbling. I wasn't sure what had gotten into them with all of this good behavior, but I definitely was not going to complain. As they got dressed and ready for school, I headed back to the kitchen to finish breakfast. Liam was awake now and was folding his blankets on the couch. He came into the kitchen when he saw me.

"Good morning." He leaned down to kiss me. "I snuck down to the couch an hour or so ago just in case the girls got up earlier than I did. Apparently, I fell back asleep. Your couch is pretty comfortable, although I definitely prefer your bed. I didn't want the girls to find me upstairs. It would ruin our good reputation. "

"Great thinking. We wouldn't want a bad reputation." I smiled, thinking again how thoughtful he was.

"What can I help you do in here?" Liam grabbed a coffee mug from the cupboard and filled it to the top.

"Absolutely nothing. You took care of dinner last night, so breakfast is on me. You have the morning off." I smiled, turning back to the stove so I didn't burn the eggs.

"In that case, I'm going to shower. I'll be down in a few minutes." Liam headed upstairs.

A couple minutes later, the girls were seated at the table devouring their breakfast. They asked where Liam was, and Rose hadn't failed to comment on the blankets which were neatly folded on the couch. The girls ate, carried their dishes to the sink, and grabbed their backpacks. I walked them outside to catch the bus. As I was cleaning up the kitchen, I heard Liam coming downstairs.

"I have some food for you if you're hungry."

"I'm starving, thanks." He dug heartily into the plate I put in front of him.

"It was nice having you here last night. It's the safest I've felt in a long time. I want to thank you." I looked Liam in the eye to be sure he knew how much I meant it.

"Not necessary. There's no place I'd rather be, Emma. Besides, protecting you gives me a great excuse to shack up with you."

"Oh, really? Is that what we're doing? Shacking up?" I feigned irritation.

"Well, yeah, looks that way to me." Liam shrugged.

"Well, if last night is any indication of what "shacking up" with you is like, then I'm all for it," I giggled.

Just then, my cellphone rang. I grabbed it off of the counter, cringing when I saw the display register "Unavailable." Seeing the number, my hopes were dashed that the stranger was finished with me. Liam noticed the look on my face as I answered the phone.

"Hello," I said tentatively.

"Good morning, Emma," the stranger said. "I

noticed last night you had a house guest."

"What do you want? Why don't you just leave me alone?" I demanded angrily.

Liam walked toward me and grabbed the phone from my hand.

"Who is this?" he demanded in his most authoritative voice.

Liam moved the phone away from his ear and irritably hit the "End" button.

"There's no one there. He already hung up." Liam angrily ran his hands through his hair, his frustration apparent.

"I hate this. I hate knowing that I'm being watched. What does he want from me? I don't have any idea what he's looking for," I was on the verge of tears once again.

Liam wrapped his arms around me, soothingly rubbing my back.

"I'm going to find out who he is and what he wants. I promise you. Why don't you go upstairs and get ready for work? I'll work from here today, so I can walk you next door then come back. No arguments."

I obediently went upstairs to shower and get ready for work, feeling like a deflated balloon. Dealing with customers was the last thing I wanted to do today, but I didn't have a choice. I was expecting a big shipment, and I couldn't leave Jane alone to deal with it all. Besides, working might keep my mind off of what was going on.

Once I was ready to go, Liam escorted me next door. I felt like a child being walked to school by a parent. It seemed ridiculous to be walked ten feet from my house to work, but Liam insisted and I wasn't up for an argument. I felt like I was no longer in control of my life. Liam kissed me goodbye and headed back to the house, promising to come fetch me at the end of the day.

Jane looked at me inquisitively as I entered Morning Glory, but didn't ask the questions I knew she was dying to. I smiled weakly and headed back to my office, shut my door, sat at my desk, and broke down and cried.

***

Once I had myself under control, I set about readying the stock room for the shipment that was due anytime. I just had to stay busy. That was the key. I couldn't be dissolving into tears every five minutes, even if I felt like it.

"Emma, the truck is here," Jane said, poking her head around the door of the stock room.

"Okay. Things are ready back here. You can tell the delivery guy to bring it on back," I said, refusing to meet Jane's eyes. I knew if I looked at her and saw compassion and concern I would lose it again.

The rest of the afternoon seemed to crawl by at a snail's pace. I kept busy, but the hands on the clock seemed to not be moving. Finally, three-thirty arrived, and so did Liam to walk me home.

We met the bus as we had the day before, got the girls started on their homework, and I began dinner. Liam was helping Lily with a Math problem when his cellphone rang. He glanced at the display, excused himself, and went outside to take the phone call.

A few minutes later, he came back inside looking grim. I wondered what was wrong.

"Emma, can I speak with you upstairs, please?" Liam asked. He headed up the stairs and I followed, trying to imagine what was going on.

"What's up?" I shut the bedroom door behind me.

"That was a call from work. I need to send in a file to my boss and it's on my home computer. I have to go to my house in order to send it, and he needs it by tonight." Liam raked his hands through his hair. I couldn't help observe he did this when he was nervous and frustrated. I was learning his body language.

"Okay..." I wasn't sure why this was such a big

deal. I obviously did not understand the problem.

"I don't want to leave you alone, but I have to do this. It's going to take me a couple of hours. Maybe you can all just come with me," Liam said hopefully.

"Is that all? I thought it was something serious." I breathed a sigh of relief. "The girls and I will be fine here for a couple of hours, Liam. I think it's best to stick to the routine as much as possible for the girls' sakes. We don't want them knowing something is wrong. I'll be sure that the doors are all locked, and you're just going to be across town if I need you."

Liam didn't look convinced, but we both knew he had little choice in the matter. He had work to do, and he needed to do it. I convinced him that we would be perfectly fine inside of my locked house in the middle of the afternoon. He told me he would be back as soon as possible, but I noticed the anxiety on his face as he headed toward the front door. Liam grabbed his car keys and headed out, giving me strict instructions to keep everything locked and to not answer the door. He was so nervous about leaving me for a couple of hours, and I felt guilty for putting him under so much stress.

I settled in on the couch to watch a movie and wait for Liam to get back. The girls were playing dolls upstairs, and instead of doing chores, I opted for some down time. I flipped through the channels and saw that *Casablanca* was just starting. It was one of my favorite old movies, and it would keep me well occupied for a while. I hadn't seen *Casablanca* for years, and it was so romantic. I knew it would be the perfect distraction. I was about halfway through the movie when my phone rang. I assumed it was Liam, and answered on the first ring. I quickly realized my mistake.

"Home alone, I see," the stranger said.

"What do you want?" Not really knowing what else to say to the man. I wished I knew what I could say to him to stop him from harassing me. If I could only convince him I didn't know what he thought I knew.

"You know what I want. You are testing my patience. Things would be much better for you if you would just tell me where I can find them." There was a frantic tone to his voice I hadn't heard before. This was probably a bad sign. He was obviously getting desperate for information he thought I had, and my refusal was angering him even further.

"I told you before I don't know what you're talking about." Why wouldn't he believe me?

"You know more than you're letting on. Your boyfriend knows what I want too. Perhaps you should ask him. There are a lot of things you don't know about Liam O'Reilly. I'm warning you. You'll be sorry," the stranger said right before the line went dead.

I sat on the couch staring at my phone. What did Liam know? The man said Liam was keeping secrets. Did this man know Liam?

I'm sure there were a lot of things I didn't know about Liam, but were they things that were somehow connected to these phone calls and invasions of my privacy? Was it possible he had a connection to my stalker? I had a hard time believing Liam harbored secrets that would put me in danger.

A million thoughts swirled around in my head, but they were interrupted when my phone rang again. I glanced at the display, and breathed a sigh of relief seeing it was Liam. He told me that he was on his way home and he would just use his key to come in, so not to panic when I heard the front door open.

When he came into the living room, he immediately knew that something was wrong. He sat down on the couch next to me.

"What happened?" Liam cut to the chase.

"He called again. He knew you weren't here, which

means he's watching me, us."

"What did he say this time?" Liam tried hard not to show his anger.

"He said he was running out of patience with me and he knew I had what he wanted. He said you knew what he wanted too, and there were a lot of things I didn't know about you. Do you think this man knows you, Liam?" I searched his face for reassurance that it wasn't true.

To my dismay, Liam seemed unsurprised that the man had mentioned him, and it occurred to me that his lack of astonishment was strange. I wasn't sure what was going on, but could it somehow be tied to Liam? I didn't want to believe it could, but the bad feeling in the pit of my stomach was back. Maybe it had something to do with a case he was involved in. Maybe he had made someone angry and they were hoping to hurt him through me. I didn't know how, but I needed to find out who this stalker was.

"Emma, I will take care of you. I don't want you to worry." He put his arm around me. At that moment, my intuition told me Liam knew more than he was letting on.

Deep down, I didn't believe Liam would purposely endanger me or the girls. His intentions were good, and I loved him fiercely, but I realized what was going on could be connected to him. As much as I didn't want to intrude on his privacy, I was determined to find out the truth. My life and the lives of my children depended on it.

Chapter Twenty-Five

I awoke the next morning with a plan securely formulated in my head. I had thought all night long about how I could get away from Liam and his babysitting long enough to do some research into his past. I originally planned to take today off, but decided going to the shop would give me the privacy I needed for sleuthing. If Liam believed I was working, he would be content to leave me alone for the day. I would go into my office and surf the Internet for information on Liam and his FBI career.

Quite honestly, I didn't even know what I was looking for. I wasn't sure what I would find, but I was hoping he wasn't involved in something that had put the girls and me in danger. I didn't know what I would do if I found out he was.

I headed to the bathroom for a quick shower. I stood under the steaming water, uneasy about my decision. I didn't want to snoop into Liam's past, but he didn't leave me much choice. He wasn't exactly forthcoming with personal information, and if something he was working on for a case was in some way connected to the man who was harassing me, I deserved to know.

I dried myself off, quickly got dressed, and headed to wake up the girls. Liam was still sleeping, and that was fine with me. The less interaction I had with him this morning, the better. I didn't want him to pick up on my anxiety, which was pretty high at this point. Plus, I was a terrible liar and he would see right through me.

I fixed the girls a quick breakfast and got them out of the house and off to school. I cleaned up the kitchen, trying to move quietly. I snuck back upstairs and saw that Liam was still out. Deciding that it was for the best, I left him a note telling him I had things I needed to finish up at work today. He would probably be angry with me for not waking him up to walk me next door, but I would deal with that later.

I walked into work and Jane looked up from the coffee she was making.

"What are you doing here? Isn't this your day off?"

"It is. I have some work I need to do on the computer, though, and thought I might get more accomplished here in my office than at home." I hoped the questions would stop there.

"Okay. I won't bother you then." Jane smiled. She looked at me curiously, and I'm sure she knew I was up to something.

"Thanks, Jane." I headed back to my office. I breathed a sigh of relief that I didn't have to explain. I had quite a guilty conscience.

Closing the door behind me, I settled in at my desk. I was nervous. I didn't want to intrude on Liam's privacy, but I didn't see any other way to find out what I needed to know. I prayed I didn't find out anything bad, because I didn't want to have to deal with the ramifications.

I did a quick Google search for "Liam O'Reilly" and came up with about ten pages of results. All of them couldn't pertain to my Liam, I hoped. Just in case, I narrowed it down a bit. I typed in "Liam O'Reilly, Chicago" and managed to cut the search results in half. I began clicking on results. There were quite a few articles relating to his stellar FBI career.

I discovered he had won several awards, and had been recognized many times for bravery. He had been involved in high profile cases during his time with the Bureau. He was impressively accomplished. I felt a surge of pride for the man I loved.

I continued clicking through results, perusing page after page of news articles. Nothing seemed out of place. I certainly didn't find anything even remotely related to negative activity involving him. I didn't find anything which spoke about problems or issues with any of the cases that he had worked on.

I immediately felt ashamed of myself. I was the worst girlfriend ever. I could have kicked myself for prying into Liam's past. What was I thinking? Of course there wasn't anything bad to find. He was a good man. I was about to close out of the search results when something caught my eye. I saw the headline "FBI Agent Nearly Catches Jewel Thieves" on the last page of search results. Curiosity got the better of me, and I continued to read. I read the entire article through twice, not able to believe what I was seeing the first time. My hands began to shake, and I thought I was going to pass out. It couldn't be true, could it?

I glanced at the article again, needing to read it one more time just to be sure. I looked at the date and noticed the article was written six years ago. An FBI agent named Liam O'Reilly investigated the case of a big-time jewel thief. The thing that made this case interesting was the primary jewel thief was a woman who had been stealing for years. She had pilfered close to a billion dollars' worth of jewelry during the course of her career. The woman's name was Veronica Smith. The article speculated Veronica Smith had a male partner, a man she was supposedly intimately involved with, and the FBI agent in charge of the case had been extremely close to catching the duo.

According to the article, he had been in Canada waiting for Veronica and her partner's plane to land. I went on to read Agent O'Reilly had all of the proof he needed, and was waiting to apprehend them. In an event that was completely coincidental, the plane had crashed. With the primary suspects dead, the case remained open. There was a quote from Agent O'Reilly that said, "I will not rest until this case is solved. It might take me years to recover the jewels, but you can rest assured I will."

I closed my laptop and sat at my desk. I was stunned and try as I might, I couldn't piece it all together in my mind. Liam had been investigating Veronica. Veronica had been a jewelry thief? The man thought to be Veronica's partner had to be Jacob. My husband had been a criminal? I had been married to a jewelry thief?

Unbelievable. Worse, Liam had known about Jacob and Veronica long before I ever met him. He knew all along about me. He knew more about my life than I did. He knew everything from the beginning. When he had asked me my life story and I had spilled it all out, he knew.

I sat there dumbfounded. I felt completely betrayed. I fell for him and his deception. I must be the world's biggest idiot. He wasn't interested in me. He got close to me to learn more about Jacob. Liam didn't love me. He was only interested in me and my connection with Jacob and Veronica. I was his only hope of finding out information. He was using me to solve the case. The article said he wouldn't give up, until the case was closed? He was obviously still investigating, and I was his main source of information.

All of the events of the past couple of months raced through my head: Liam buying Veronica's house, Liam coming into Morning Glory and trying to get close to me, Liam making me fall in love with him. I couldn't believe all of the lies and all of the deception. I had fallen for it all. I must be the dumbest woman on the planet to have been so completely swindled by two different men.

My stomach churned, and I thought I was going to be sick. How was it possible that I felt more betrayed now than I had when I found out about Jacob's affair with Veronica? Even discovering that my husband was a jewel thief and had been leading a double life didn't make me feel this betrayed.

What made this so gut-wrenching was I truly loved Liam. It hurt so much more with him because I had given him my whole heart. I hadn't held anything back from him. I allowed him to see all of my fears and vulnerabilities. I trusted him fully and completely, and all the time he had been deceiving me. I gave him my heart and he was lying the whole time. He was dishonest with me, and worse, dishonest with my girls. That was unforgivable.

I sat at my desk for over an hour, trying to figure out what I was going to do. One thing I knew for sure was Liam obviously had to go. I could not even stand to think about seeing him again, and he was living in my house. How was I going to face him? I had no idea what I was going to tell the girls, and decided for now, I would make something up. I couldn't bear to think of the hurt they would feel when they realized Liam would no longer be a part of our lives, but I needed to take action now. I steeled myself for what I had to do and rose from my desk.

I told Jane I needed to go home, and with trembling hands, I opened the front door of my house. Liam was sitting at the kitchen counter working on his laptop. He stood up to greet me when he saw me come into the kitchen. One look at my face, and he took a step back.

"Emma, what's wrong?" Liam reached out to take my hand.

At his touch, I pulled my hand away as though I had placed it on a hot burner. I couldn't stand for him to be near me. I willed myself to only think of the anger. I would need it to mask the fact that my world was disintegrating.

"Get your hands off me. How could you?" The tremble in my voice echoed in my ears. I was on the verge of tears, but I was trying my best not to break down in front of him. I would not crumble right now. He had seen enough weakness from me.

"Emma, what are you talking about? What happened?"

"You lied to me from the very beginning. Was this some kind of joke to you? Was it a game to see how quickly I would fall for you? Did you enjoy watching me be an idiot?" My voice rose in anger with each question.

"Slow down and tell me what's going on. I don't know what you're talking about."

"Don't you, Detective O'Reilly? Does the name Veronica Smith ring a bell? It seems to me you knew Veronica Smith long before I told you about her. You obviously knew who she was since you're living in her house!" I screamed. "How could you do this to me?"

Liam's face fell. If I had any doubts, in that instant I knew it was all true. He couldn't deny it, and to his credit, he didn't try to.

"Emma, please just listen to me. Yes, it's true, but you have to believe I love you."

"Love me? Really? This is your definition of love? Dishonesty and lies? I had that with Jacob! I don't want that kind of love," My words were as sharp as knives as I spat them out.

"Okay, please let me explain. When I first came here, I did want to get to know you because I thought you might share something with me that could shed some light on the case. I thought you knew about Jacob. But when I got to know you that thought immediately flew out the window. I love you Emma. I love you and that has nothing to do with the case. I should have told you about my connection to Jacob and Veronica from the beginning, but I was afraid you wouldn't give me a chance."

"A chance? That's exactly what I gave you! I told you I didn't trust men. I told you how hurt I had been, and yet you just continued on, luring me in, making me love you..." I broke off, my body shaking with sobs I couldn't hold in any longer. I swear I could literally feel my heart breaking inside of me it hurt so badly.

Seeing me crying, Liam walked over and tried to put his arms around me. I jerked away.

"Do not touch me. Ever again. Get your things and get out of my house. I never want to see you again," I said through clenched teeth.

"Emma, you don't mean that. You're just angry with me. I can't leave you here alone. You might be in danger," Liam pleaded with me.

"I'll take the danger. Get out now. You have five minutes to gather up your things and get out of my house," I said coldly.

Liam looked at me in disbelief. He walked slowly upstairs and gathered his things. A few minutes later, he came back into the kitchen, put his laptop in its case, and carried his bags to the front door. He came back into the kitchen.

"Emma, please listen to me." He quietly tried one more time. "I love you."

"I'm through listening to you. Goodbye, Liam." I turned my back to him.

"This is not over, Emma." Liam gathered his bags and walked out my front door.

The minute the door closed behind him, I ran upstairs to my room and threw myself onto my bed. The room still smelled of Liam's cologne. I could almost feel him in here. How was I going to get through this? I felt like the life had been sucked out of me. My entire body hurt. I laid my head down on the pillow that Liam had slept on and cried myself to sleep.

***

Liam drove home on auto-pilot. He pulled into his driveway, unsure how he got there. He turned off the vehicle, but didn't get out. His mind was a million miles away, his only focus on how to fix this mess with Emma. He had never seen her so angry. He didn't even believe she was capable of such fury. How had she found out about his past?

This was the outcome he had feared most. He knew from the start if Emma found out the secret on her own it was over. With every ounce of his being he wished he had made the choice from the beginning to tell her.

Emma and the girls were his future. He believed that whole-heartedly. Whatever the cost, he would win them back. He would spend the rest of his life proving to her that his feelings were real, if that's what it took.

He angrily slammed his fists on the steering wheel. He was so stupid! He had happiness in the palm of his hands and had blown it. He should have told her the truth and trusted their love would be enough to see them through. Instead, he had deceived her and betrayed her. Now, she had banished him from her life. The way she refused to look at him when he left ripped his heart from his chest.

He would win her trust again. Right now, though, the most important thing was keeping her and the girls safe. He knew that they were in danger. He hadn't quite pieced the puzzle together, but he knew he was close. If Emma didn't want him near her, he would just have to find another way to protect her. Determined, he turned the car back on and pulled out of the driveway.

Chapter Twenty-Six

When I awoke, I looked at the clock. It was two-thirty in the afternoon. I had only an hour until the girls would be home. I had to pull it together for them. I could not be weak and weepy when they saw me. I headed into the bathroom and splashed some water on my face. I looked at myself in the mirror. My eyes were puffy and swollen from all of the crying. I got out my concealer and applied some under my eyes. It helped a little bit. I thought it was enough that the girls wouldn't notice.

I felt empty inside. For weeks, I had been gliding along on a cloud of happiness, and now I landed, or rather I dropped, back to earth. I didn't know how I was going to cope with this. I had envisioned a future with Liam in it, and now that future looked bleak. If it weren't for my girls, I would just curl up in a ball and sleep for the next week. Mothers didn't have the option of checking out, though, so I had to stay strong.

The girls had always been the driving force that kept me going, and that's what I had to remember. I had to be tough for them. They were going to be confused about Liam not being here and I needed to come up with a good excuse. I decided that I would just tell them he was having some repairs done on his house and he needed to be there for a while to supervise the work. I didn't think they would question that. At least I hoped not, since I didn't think I could handle their questions.

I straightened up the house a bit and started my daily loads of laundry. I just had to stay busy. That was how I was going to get through this. I had made it through my fair share of hard times, and I was trying to convince myself I could make it through this too. I wandered around the house inventing chores that needed done. At three-thirty, I headed outside to meet the bus.

The girls jumped off the bus and came running over

to where I was standing in the front yard.

"Hi Mom," said Lily, looking at me curiously. Lily was pretty discerning, and if any of the girls were going to see through my act, it would be her.

"Hey, honey," I plastered a smile on my face, feigning a happiness I definitely didn't feel.

I gave all three girls a hug as we headed inside. I told myself I only needed to keep up the façade until they were in bed, and then I could crumble. I could do anything for a few hours, right?

Deciding dinner preparation was beyond my abilities today, I picked up the phone and ordered a pizza. The girls were thrilled of course, and I was glad they were happy.

We continued through our afternoon, each of us busy and wrapped up in our own duties. I almost thought I was off the hook explaining where Liam was, but that was wishful thinking.

"Mama, where's Liam? Why isn't he here today?" Rose questioned. I took a deep breath, hoping to steady my voice before I spoke.

"Well, Liam has some work to do on his house, some repairs that need to be finished. He has to be there to oversee them, so he won't be around for a while," I made sure to keep my back to them while I told the lie. I was a horrible liar, and knew my girls would see right through me.

"Is everything okay?" Dahlia asked.

"Yeah, honey, it's all good. Liam just has some things to take care of right now," I hoped my voice sounded nonchalant.

Content that I was telling them the truth, they dropped the subject. That had been easier than I anticipated. Thank goodness. I knew I wasn't up to discussing Liam any more than I absolutely had to. I was trying not to think about him, but I was finding that impossible as well. The truth was even though I was angry and hurt, I still loved him. That was something I didn't think I would ever get over.

It wasn't long until I heard a knock at the front door, signaling the arrival of our pizza. I grabbed my wallet and headed to the door to pay the delivery man. The girls devoured the pizza, and I sent them up to bathe and get into pajamas while I cleaned up the mess.

A while later, I was sitting on Rose's bed reading her favorite book, *Sophie Gets A Pet*. It didn't seem to matter how many times I read it to her, she never got tired of it. To be honest, I never got tired of it either. The routine calmed my frazzled nerves. I kissed all three girls goodnight and headed back downstairs.

My cellphone rang, and my stomach dropped. With all that had happened today, I had completely forgotten about the stranger. This was just what I needed, something else to be stressed about, especially since I was alone again. I walked over to my phone and glanced at the display, expecting to see "Unavailable." Instead, I saw that it was Liam.

If I were being honest with myself, all I really wanted was to pick up the phone and hear his voice. My heart ached. How could I still love him so much after what he had done to me? I knew I couldn't talk to him no matter how much I wanted to. I wished I could forget that stupid article. I wished I could again be oblivious to the fact that my dead husband was a thief and the man I loved was investigating him. I wanted to go back to yesterday when my life had been so close to perfect. As tempted as I was at this moment to do just that, I knew that I couldn't. If I couldn't trust Liam, we had no future. He had betrayed me, and he didn't deserve my trust or the fierce love I felt for him. I picked up my phone and declined the call. I headed upstairs to my room, and fell asleep in my bed that suddenly felt too big and too empty.

Chapter Twenty-Seven

A week passed by uneventfully. Liam called me several times every day, and each time, I declined the call. I couldn't talk to him. I couldn't let down my guard for a second. I knew if I heard his voice, all of my resolve would crumble and I would go running back to him. I refused to be weak. He had lied to me. He had used me for information. I trusted him and he deceived me. In my mind, it was unforgivable.

That knowledge didn't make my heart hurt any less. I went through each day feeling like a zombie. I had no energy and I felt like the walking dead. Even though the girls didn't ask, I could see the way they looked at me. They knew something was very wrong.

It felt as if the life had been sucked right out of me. I hadn't felt this empty when Jacob died, or when my parents passed away. I thought nothing could send me reeling like the deaths of my parents, but Liam's betrayal and subsequent removal from my life plunged me into depths of sorrow I hadn't experienced before.

The only thing that kept me putting one foot in front of the other was the girls. I had to put on a good front for them. Overall, I think I had done a decent job. I was still getting out of bed each day. I was still running a business. I was still managing to take care of the girls.

Interestingly enough, the stranger had not called since Liam had been gone. I'm not sure if there was a connection or not, but I breathed a sigh of relief that I didn't have to deal with him anymore. Apparently, he decided to leave me alone. He must have realized I didn't know anything about what he was looking for and moved on.

One thing I looked forward to was Sadie coming home today. She had been gone for two weeks, and I missed her terribly. I wasn't looking forward to telling her about Liam and me, but I knew she would stand by me as always. I needed her strength. She was coming for dinner tonight, and I was glad I would be able to unload on her.

I drained the pasta I was cooking for dinner as I heard the front door open. Placing the pot back on the stove, I drizzled a little olive oil into the pan so the noodles wouldn't stick together. Sadie came in the front door and the girls eagerly greeted her. They had missed her too.

I hadn't told Sadie about me and Liam. I didn't think I could do that over the phone. I knew myself well enough to know that if I started telling her what was going on, I would be a mess. As a result of my lack of information, Sadie was surprised when she saw me.

I knew I wasn't looking my best. The situation had taken a toll on me physically as well. I had dark circles under my eyes and my skin was even more pale than usual. I had no appetite and hadn't eaten well in a week. I was nauseous most days, and had even vomited a couple of times from the stress. The girls hadn't asked questions about the changes in my appearance. Maybe they were perceptive enough to know I didn't want to talk about it. Sadie knew something was very wrong with me the minute she saw me, though.

"Hey munchkins, I have presents for you guys. Why don't you open them while I catch up with your mom?" She handed them each a bag of gifts.

"Thanks Aunt Sadie," the girls cried excitedly, settling themselves in the family room with their bags.

Sadie took my hand and led me into the kitchen, closing the door behind us so the girls wouldn't hear. True to form, Sadie didn't begin by asking me questions. She just grabbed me, hugging me fiercely. That was all I needed for the waterworks to set in. I sobbed, my entire body shaking, while she just held me. Sadie and I had been through so much together that there were times we didn't need words. I cried for a few minutes, and then managed to get myself under control. I sat down at the kitchen table, knowing I needed to explain things.

"I'm going to go in the family room and check on the girls. They'll be excited about their gifts, and I don't want them to come in here and see you like this. Pull yourself together and I'll be back. I want to know what happened," Sadie said, giving me instructions. I was grateful to her for taking charge. She always knew exactly what I needed.

I took a few deep breaths and tried to push away the nausea. I probably just needed to eat something, but the thought of food was more than I could handle. I couldn't seem to shake it. I knew it was because of stress.

I managed to get control of my emotions as Sadie walked back into the kitchen. She sat down at the table opposite me and took my hand. I knew I would feel some relief once I told her. She had seen me through many horrible situations, but this was the worst.

"Em, I don't know what's happened, but I'm guessing it's something with Liam. I've seen you down before, but I've never seen you like this. I'm really worried about you. You look like you've been through hell and back. Tell me how I can help you." Sadie squeezed my hand.

I told her the entire story. I told her how close Liam and I had become. I told her how much I loved him, and how we started talking about a future together. I told her about the stranger who had begun harassing me, and how Liam had moved in to protect us. Then I told her about my discovery of Liam's connection to Veronica and Jacob, and how I had found out he had been using me. Sadie was shocked, as I had been, to learn my late husband was a jewelry thief. I told her Liam had lied and used me and deceived me. After I finished, Sadie sat there quietly, processing it all. I could see she was thinking very carefully before she spoke. Finally, she looked me right in the eyes.

"Emma, I know you think Liam betrayed you. I'll admit, he could have handled this differently, but I do not believe for one second his feelings for you are anything but genuine. I've seen the two of you together, and the man loves you. He loves your girls. I won't believe anything else," Sadie sounded completely convinced that this was the truth.

"He lied to me. You know how important the truth is. I can't trust him. If I can't trust him, then I can't be with him," I said stubbornly.

"I can see you aren't in any position to hear me right now, and that's okay. You're hurt, and rightfully so. I just want you to think long and hard about this. No matter what he did, Liam loves you. I'm as sure of that as I have ever been about anything." Sadie squeezed my hand reassuringly.

I didn't respond. I couldn't open my heart up to Liam even a little bit. He had lied to me. He had used me. I kept repeating this mantra in my head, sure that I would believe it if I kept saying it. Nothing else mattered besides that. If you loved someone, you didn't lie to them. That was the one thing I was sure of. I wouldn't forgive Liam. End of story.

"I have an idea." Sadie let go of my hand. "I know you've been holding it together in front of the girls for over a week now. What you really need is some time alone to fall apart. You need some time to think about things and work it all out in your head. I've missed the girls terribly, and would love to have some girl time with them. How about I take them and that pasta upstairs to my place and we can have dinner and they can sleep over? You can catch up on some sleep and decompress."

"Thank you Sadie. I think that's exactly what I need. I have been miserable the past week, and it might be nice just to wallow in some self-pity for a night without having to put on a happy face for the girls." I gave her a hug. This was one of the many reasons she was my best friend. She got me. She knew what I needed without me ever having to ask for it.

I told the girls to go upstairs and pack an overnight bag for Sadie's. I didn't have to tell them twice. They were pretty excited, to say the least. I placed the pasta in a box for Sadie to carry upstairs. She hugged me goodbye, telling me to rest. I said that I would try. I kissed the girls and told them to behave. They were so excited for some time with Sadie they didn't even question the change in plans.

A few minutes later, I was alone, the quietness of the house settling around me. For once, I didn't mind. I didn't have to be anything for anyone right now. I could just be. I was exhausted, to say the least. It was only five-thirty in the afternoon, but I felt like I could crawl into bed and sleep for two days. I decided to shower, put on my nightgown, and curl up in my bed with a movie. I could cry if I wanted to. I could sleep if I wanted to. I could get angry if I wanted to. I could do whatever I wanted to do. The problem was that the only thing I really wanted to do was call Liam.

Ignoring that longing, I headed upstairs for my shower. After I was finished, I put on my comfiest, rattiest nightgown. I looked in the mirror and decided that I definitely looked horrible. There was no question about it. Luckily, no one was going to see me tonight. I climbed into bed and flipped my television on, surfing the channels mindlessly for a couple of minutes. Nothing really jumped out at me. I missed Liam so badly it physically hurt. My body felt like I had been run over by a truck. How was it possible to miss him this much? Hadn't I been a perfectly functioning woman before I met him? Well, maybe not perfectly functioning, but close.

I replayed the last week in my mind for the hundredth time. Had I been hasty to break things off with him? Maybe I should have listened to his side of the story.

Maybe if I had let him explain things to me they may have made more sense. Was there an explanation good enough for what he had done? No, I had to stand firm on this. I could not be with a man who had used me. He didn't deserve my forgiveness.

I flipped through the channels a little longer and saw that one of my all-time favorite movies was about to begin. I turned the channel where *Pretty Woman* was just starting. This would be a good choice. I could laugh and cry at someone else's problems, hopefully forgetting about mine for a while.

I settled into my fluffy pillows and pulled the blankets over me. I was so tired, and I didn't feel well. I tried to focus my brain on the movie instead of the nausea, and lost myself for a bit. About halfway through, I could feel myself getting drowsy. My eyes grew heavy, and instead of fighting it, I gave in to blissful sleep.

***

I opened my eyes and they adjusted to my bedroom, which was now completely dark. I glanced at the clock beside my bed and noticed that it was 9:30 p.m. I had been asleep for a couple of hours, and was still exhausted. It was a good thing Sadie had the girls with her. I could take advantage of the empty house and catch up on my sleep. I turned off the television and rolled over, snuggling into my bed. I was about to doze off again when I thought I heard something downstairs. I listened for a minute and didn't hear it again. It was probably just the house settling, so I went back to sleep.

***

My eyes flew open as I felt a large hand cover my mouth. I was so stunned that I froze. What was going on? I blinked several times, certain I was dreaming. This was obviously a nightmare. I tried to adjust my vision to the blackness of my room. I managed to turn my head just enough to look at the clock and saw it was 3:00 in the morning. I tried not to panic, but that was nearly impossible. I couldn't see anything, and there was definitely a hand covering my mouth. My brain finally registered the situation and I struggled against the hand, trying to scream, but it was useless. A large body sat down on the bed beside me, leaning on me so I couldn't move. Terror coursed through my entire being. I had no idea what was happening, but this was certainly real. It wasn't a dream as I had thought when I first opened my eyes.

"We meet at last Emma," said the man.

As soon as he spoke, I knew he was the man from the phone calls. As I recognized his voice, panic consumed me. My first thought was I was going to die tonight. The stalker hadn't given up as I had so stupidly assumed. He was lulling me into a false sense of security so he was able to completely take me by surprise. I hadn't received any phone calls in over a week, so I had let my guard down. Had I even locked my front door before I came upstairs earlier? I thought hard to remember, but I couldn't.

I tried to calm myself. The more I struggled, the worse it would be for me. I willed myself to stay calm. My heart beat wildly in my chest and I had a hard time controlling my breathing with his hand over my mouth. I tried to breathe slowly so I didn't hyperventilate, but it was difficult. I made myself lay still and quiet, and kept repeating in my head that I would not scream.

"I'm having a hard time seeing your pretty face in the dark, Emma," the man said. "I'm going to turn on a light, but to do that, I have to take my hand off of your mouth. It would be in your best interest not to scream."

I nodded my head. I was going to do exactly what he asked me to do. Cooperation was my only hope of getting out alive. I thought of my girls and knew I had to do whatever this man said if I ever wanted to see them again.

He turned on the bedside lamp and I saw him for the first time. I'm not sure what I expected, but he was definitely not the type of guy I anticipated. I guess I had been expecting a derelict, and he was quite the opposite. He was very tall and muscular. He was quite handsome and well-dressed. If I had seen him in my coffee shop, I would have been attracted to him. He had a quality that was charismatic, and I imagined a great many women were drawn to him. He was the kind of man who was probably used to women throwing themselves at him.

He had on a leather jacket and black leather gloves. I suddenly realized that the gloves were to prevent him from leaving fingerprints in my house. That thought had me panicking all over again, and rethinking my game plan. Was it a bad idea to do what he said? Maybe I should fight back. Cooperating might be too dangerous for me. Who knew what he might ask me to do? I made a split-second decision that escaping was the better plan. His back was turned to me and I thought he might be doing something on his phone. Now was the time to try and get away.

He still hadn't turned around, so I mustered all of my courage and leaped off of the bed. I sprinted toward my open bedroom door. I thought if I could just get out of this room I could hide somewhere else in the house. I had underestimated how quickly he could move. He reached me in a split second. From the angry look on his face, I had made the wrong choice. He looked as if he might actually kill me on the spot.

Instead, he grabbed me by the hair and threw me on my bed. He slapped me hard across the face. I could feel the blood trickling from my lip down my chin. I couldn't tell how badly my lip was cut, but there was a lot of blood. I grabbed my sheet and tried to staunch the flow. He stood there, looming above me. I wasn't sure if he was going to hit me again, so I tried to stay as still as I could. My attempted escape had been a terrible idea.

"That was a mistake. I didn't come here to hurt you, but I can't have you trying to leave. We are going to get to know each other very well tonight. One way or another, I will find out all that you know," he leaned down toward me.

His face was only an inch from mine. I didn't know what he was going to do next, but I was terrified to find out. My lip was still bleeding, although it had slowed down a bit. I could taste the saltiness as the blood trickled into my mouth.

"I should introduce myself. My name is Xavier," the man said as he closed the gap between us and kissed me roughly, licking the blood that still trailed down my lip.

Chapter Twenty-Eight

I didn't move as he continued to kiss me. The sudden horrible realization of exactly what his intentions were for me tonight hit me. He grabbed my hair and tilted my head back and I had no choice but to let him do it. I was a puppet in his hands, and he was the cruel puppet master. Images of my daughters played like a movie in my head. I had to be smart. The girls had already lost a father. I could not let them lose their mother too.

Xavier's free hand trailed down to my thin nightgown which he grabbed and pulled on so hard it ripped. My naked body was exposed. My mind began to race of all the ways he could hurt and torture me. I had never felt such terror in my life. My fear was a living, breathing thing. My lip still bled slowly, and was now dripping down onto my chest. I knew better than to move, even to try and stop the bleeding.

"You're a lovely woman," Xavier said softly, taking in my naked form. "I have no intention of harming you if you cooperate. I merely came here to get to know you better. I have so enjoyed our phone calls. You should be aware, however, that I have a very bad temper, and I don't like it when my rules are not followed. I've been told before I need to learn to control my anger. I just can't seem to, though."

I had learned my lesson. I was prepared to accept any demands he made. I would do anything as long as I got out of this alive.

"You're going to come downstairs with me. You're a feisty one. I need a way to contain you. I can't take the chance of you trying to run again." He never took his eyes off of me.

"I won't run." My voice trembled, and my heart raced in my chest.

"For some reason I don't believe you." He laughed,

and for a moment he didn't seem quite as threatening. The moment passed quickly, though, and I saw the cold look come back into his steel-grey eyes.

Xavier had my hair clamped tightly in his hand and I couldn't move my head. He let go and grabbed both my arms, roughly pulling me up to a standing position. The shreds of my nightgown fell to the floor. A hungry look crossed his face as he stared at my body. I knew what was likely to happen if his gaze lingered too long, and I knew I had to distract him. I could not let him violate me that way. I would never recover from it.

"I'm cold. Can I please have my robe? I'll do whatever you want, but let me cover up," I pleaded, hoping to reach some part of him that might still be human.

"It seems a shame to cover up such beauty." He trailed his fingertip across my jaw, down my neck and to my collarbone. He stood there looking at me, desire in his eyes. His hands reached out to touch me. He ran his palms down my arms and back up again. My body trembled beneath his touch. A wave of nausea threatened to consume me, but I willed myself not to feel it.

"Your skin is so soft. It feels like satin. Liam is a very lucky man." His hands trailed over every inch of my naked body. My mind was consumed with horror, but I had no choice but to stand and let him.

"Where is your robe?"

"It's hanging on the back of my bathroom door. Don't worry. I'll stand right here. I promise I won't run." Thankful and surprised he decided to let me cover up.

Xavier disappeared for a second into the bathroom and came back with my robe.

"I'll just bring this downstairs with us. I'm not ready to cover you up yet. I want to look at you a while longer."

He threw my robe across his shoulder. He stood looking at me as if he were debating what he should do. He surprised me when he bent down and scooped me up into his huge arms as if I were no bigger than a child. It was awkward and terrifying to be held, almost tenderly, by my captor. I was completely at his mercy. I tried not to think of the hopelessness of my situation, and kept telling myself to just stay calm and do whatever he said. I resolved to go along with what he wanted me to do, anything, as long as it meant he left me alive. I could not die tonight.

Xavier took me through the hall and down the stairs, all without turning on a single light. I didn't know how he managed to do this without falling, especially considering he was still carrying me. He seemed to have an uncanny ability to see in the dark. He walked slowly, not in any hurry. I felt vulnerable being held so closely. He seemed to be enjoying the whole experience. He lowered his face to my hair and breathed in my scent.

"It's a shame we had to meet under such bad circumstances, Emma. I would have enjoyed sampling some of what you have to offer." Xavier stared right into my eyes as he continued past the front door and toward the kitchen, walking slowly toward his destination.

Fear gripped me. I tried to keep the terror at bay. It was useless. His intentions were blatantly clear, and I could not let that happen. I wasn't sure how to prevent it. After all, I was naked, in his arms. He was much stronger, and I had no doubt he could make me do whatever he wanted. The only thing I could think to do was distract him, to keep him talking.

"I wish I knew what you wanted from me, Xavier," Somehow I managed to keep my voice calm and steady. "I would be happy to tell you whatever you want to know if I just knew what it was."

"You know what I want. You're just playing with me. Pretending you don't know what I'm looking for. Women are all the same. They lure you in with their beauty and then do nothing but play games with your mind."

We reached the kitchen. He looked around trying to decide what to do next. He gingerly stood me on the floor. I stood with my back against his chest and his arms wrapped around my body, the soft leather of his jacket next to my skin. Despite the close contact, I was so cold, and my body shivered.

An outsider looking in might think we were lovers from the tender way he held me. His hands roamed, but he didn't say a word. I kept my eyes closed, willing myself to go somewhere else in my head. He was confusing me. I was repulsed by him, but my body betrayed me and almost enjoyed the gentle caresses. Thankfully, it ended and he stepped away from me. I opened my eyes, frightened of what he would do next.

Walking to the kitchen table, Xavier pulled one of the chairs away from it and sat me down. He dropped to his knees, kneeling in front of me. He reached into his pocket and pulled out a pair of zip ties.

"If you remain very still, these won't hurt you. Your skin is so beautiful and I wouldn't want to mark it unnecessarily." He kissed my arms and wrists. He noticed my cut lip from where he had slapped me earlier. For a moment, he almost looked sorry. He reached out and touched the wound carefully. Again, he brought his face to mine and kissed me. I was petrified of making him angry, so I didn't resist and tried not to move. I resolved to let him do whatever he wanted, but his actions were so confusing. He had been insanely irate earlier. Now, he was treating me so tenderly, as if he were my lover.

He took my right arm and pulled it behind my back. Carefully, he zip tied it to the chair post. I could feel the device tighten around my wrist and a new sense of panic set in. My instinct was to resist, but I learned earlier that only made it worse. After my right arm was secure, he repeated the process with the left. Then he pulled out another set of zip ties and did the same with my legs, cinching my ankles to the chair legs. I was trapped. He walked over and turned on the light above the stove. It didn't illuminate the entire room, but allowed me to see a little better. I had no idea what he was going to do next, but I was sure it wouldn't be good.

"This could have been so much simpler if you had just told me where they were from the beginning, Emma," Xavier paced in front of me. I could quickly tell all traces of tenderness were gone. It was like he flipped an internal switch, and the cold and terrifying look was back.

"I don't know what you mean, Xavier. I promise you, if I did, I would tell you. What are you talking about?"

He glared at me. His face contorted with rage. He stood, towering over me. I was certain he was going to hit me again.

"The jewels, Emma!" Xavier screamed the words, his voice rising. "Tell me where the jewels are!"

Understanding hit me like Xavier's slap in the face. He was somehow connected to the jewels, and to Jacob, Veronica, and Liam. The wheels turned in my brain as I quickly tried to keep up with the information it was processing. I realized the only way I had a prayer of getting out of this was to make him think I knew where they were and I would lead him to them. I was fully aware that my ability to lie was not my strong suit, but my very existence depended on making Xavier believe I was cognizant of my late husband's illegal activities.

"Oh, the jewels," I replied, keeping my voice calm. "How do you know about them?"

"I know about them because they were my idea. I taught Veronica everything I knew. When we got married, she had no idea what I was into. She just knew I had money and she liked it. I figured out pretty quickly buried beneath her beauty was a heart as cold as ice. She wasn't interested in anything except more money."

"You were married to Veronica? I knew her, you

know." I glanced up at Xavier and saw he had gone somewhere else in his head. He was remembering Veronica.

"She was so beautiful. She's the only woman I ever loved. I thought she loved me. She pretended to. She only ever loved one thing, and that was money. When she found out I was a jewelry thief, she begged me to teach her how to steal them. She told me she would be good at it because no one would suspect her, and she was right. She was far better than I ever was." I could see Xavier was lost in the past. "I only did small-time jobs. It was good money, but it wasn't enough for Veronica. She wanted more. She hatched this grand scheme to start hitting up the ultra-rich set. I told her it was too risky. She wouldn't listen. She told me that if I wouldn't help her, she would find someone who would."

Xavier was completely lost in thought now. It was almost as if he had forgotten I was there. I looked around frantically, trying to come up with a plan to get out of this. I realized my options were extremely limited, and my hopes were dashed. It was no use. I was tied up to a chair, naked. I wasn't getting out of here. I needed to keep him talking.

"That must have been very hurtful. I'm sure you loved her very deeply." I tried my best to sound sympathetic, hoping again to reach the tender side I had seen earlier.

"She left me. I came home one day and she was waiting for me at the door with her bags packed. She told me she had found a new partner, some guy named Jacob. Does that name ring a bell?" He stared at me coldly.

"Jacob was my husband." I attempted to form an alliance with my captor. "We were both betrayed, Xavier."

"Exactly. From what I heard, their partnership worked out pretty well. They managed to steal billions of dollars' worth of jewelry. The FBI was hot on their trail. Your boyfriend, Liam, thought he could catch them. He might have, too, if they hadn't died in that plane crash," Xavier continued. "My bet is you knew exactly where those jewels were. There's no way you were married to that guy and didn't know about this."

"Do you really think I knew? Think about it. What woman would stay with a husband who was sleeping with another woman and stealing with her? You're a smart man. Does that sound logical to you?" Gaining courage as I spoke. "I didn't know about Jacob and Veronica. I didn't know they were having an affair, and I certainly didn't know my husband and my neighbor were jewelry thieves."

Apparently, Xavier didn't like my response because he slapped me again, harder this time. The cut on my lip re-opened and began bleeding profusely. The blood ran down my lip and dripped onto my chest. He was angrier than before, and I knew he was going to seriously hurt me if I didn't get help. In that instant, the plan to stay compliant and agreeable was no longer going to work. He had crossed over into a very dark place, and there was no reasoning with him. Despite my earlier resolve to follow his orders, I had to do something. My limbs securely trapped, I used the only tool I had left at my disposal. I screamed as loudly as I could.

My house was huge and chances were slim, but I prayed Sadie might hear me. I screamed and kept screaming, more loudly each time. Xavier punched me hard in the face, yelling at me to shut up. I didn't listen. I kept screaming, as if my very life depended on it, because I knew that it did.

He punched me over and over again, and I could feel myself starting to lose consciousness. The room spun and I was overwhelmed with nausea. I closed my eyes to try and stop the spinning. I thought I was going to throw up, but I continued to scream for help.

Suddenly, I heard the shattering of glass. The punching stopped. The sound of heavy, running footsteps was followed by the sound of a large thud. I tried to open my eyes, but I could only see on one side.

From what I could gather, Xavier was on the floor, hands being securely cuffed behind him. He wasn't moving, and I wondered if he was dead. The last thing I saw before I completely lost consciousness was Liam, with his gun pointed at Xavier's head.

Chapter Twenty-Nine

I woke up in a hospital room. My head throbbed, and I could only see out of one eye. I reached and felt my right eye, which seemed to be swollen four times the usual size. I held my hand up in front of my right eye, and couldn't see it. Apparently, it was swollen completely shut. My lip hurt. My fingers ran over stitches. I felt disoriented and overwhelmed with relief that I was still alive. How long had I been out? It seemed I was alone. I tried to sit up, but fell back in pain. There wasn't an inch of my body that didn't hurt. Out of the corner of my left eye, since at the moment it was the only one that worked, I saw Liam asleep in the chair in the corner.

I tried hard to remember what had happened before I passed out. Vague snippets came back to me, though I couldn't get a clear picture of any of it. There was the shattering glass. Had Liam come through the window? I remembered the thud Xavier's body made as it hit the floor. Was he dead? The clearest memory was of Liam pointing his gun at Xavier as he yelled at him not to move. I tried hard to recall more, but I couldn't. Everything after that was a complete blank. I didn't even know what day it was. Were my girls okay? They had to be worried sick about me.

"Liam," I said, hoping he would hear me and wake up. His eyes opened and he sat up and quickly rushed to my side, reaching for my hand.

"Emma, you're awake." He gave me a wide smile. "How are you feeling?"

"About as good as I probably look," I attempted a smile, and then winced in pain upon pulling the stitches in my lip. "How long have I been here?"

"Not long, just since yesterday," Liam pulled the chair up to the bed. "Do you remember what happened?"

I told Liam what I remembered. I recanted the entire story up to the point where I passed out.

"Where are my girls? Are they ok?"

"The girls are fine. They're with Sadie. I talked to her this morning, and she reassured them you were fine. She'll bring them by today after school." None of this made any sense to me, and I fought to piece the nightmare together in my head.

"I don't understand. Why were you there? Don't get me wrong, I'm glad you were. But, how did you know I needed you?" I asked, finding it hard to look in Liam's eyes after everything that had happened between us.

"Emma, I knew you were in danger, and I had to find a way to protect you. I finally figured out Veronica had a crazy ex-husband and had a suspicion he might be your stalker. I camped out every night in front of your house since you kicked me out. I needed to make sure you were safe." Liam shrugged his shoulders. He appeared to be embarrassed by his admission.

I stared at him in amazement. I couldn't believe what I heard. He had parked outside of my house to keep watch over me after I had kicked him out. Had I been wrong about him? Did he really love me?

"I saw your lights go out and figured you were asleep. I must have dozed off in my car, but when I heard you scream, I knew something was wrong. By the way, you have the loudest scream of anyone I have ever heard," Liam said with a smile, trying to lighten the tense moment. "I tried the front door, but of course it was locked. I still had a key, but I left it at my house. The only option was to break the front window. When I saw what he had done to you, I wanted to kill him. I would have, too, but I knew I needed him alive to question him. You were naked and bloody and tied to the chair. I hate myself for letting that happen to you."

"Liam, you couldn't have known about this. Xavier was crazy. He was tender one minute, and then hitting me the next. He thought I knew where the jewelry was. That's what he wanted all along. When he realized I didn't know, he got insanely angry. If you hadn't come in when you did, he would have killed me. You saved my life." I reached for his hand.

"Emma, did he...." Liam trailed off, not able to say the words.

"No, he didn't," I replied, knowing exactly what he was asking.

"Thank God. If he had touched you like that, I would go kill him right now. I couldn't stand it. I'm so sorry he hurt you at all. I'm sorry I didn't protect you like I should have." The agony on his face was almost more than I could bear.

"Please don't apologize, Liam. It's over now," I said, squeezing his hand. "By the way, what's up with the jewels? Was he crazy, or were they hidden somewhere?"

"Well, once I had him in custody, I asked him a lot of questions. He let it slip Veronica had always told him if she were to steal a huge stash, she planned to hide them behind a false wall in her house. It really was a perfect plan. Surprisingly, Xavier had no idea that I bought Veronica's house. After interrogating him, I went home and found the wall. Sure enough, they were all inside. They had been right there the whole time. Finally, after almost seven years, I can say the case is closed. I called my boss and they're sending out a crew today to gather the jewelry into evidence. They'll be processed and returned to the people they were stolen from." He smiled.

I was relieved to know that the case of the stolen jewelry was solved. It was a chapter of my life I was definitely ready to close the book on. Those jewels had been the source of so much pain and trauma. I was glad they would be returned to their rightful owners.

That left only one thing, whether or not I could forgive Liam. I wasn't sure how things were going to turn out for us. He had saved my life, and I knew I loved him.

No matter what had happened or how it had come to be, I loved him. There were things I was still angry about, but they didn't seem to matter as much in light of what had happened last night.

I had almost died, and I had been given a second chance. I didn't want to waste it by being angry over something I couldn't change. The circumstances which brought us together were obviously not ideal, but the fact remained I loved him and I knew in my heart that he loved me. Yes, he had been dishonest with me about his connection to Jacob, and it might take me some time to get over that. Thanks to Liam, though, time was something I had.

I was trying to figure out how to put my feelings into words when the door to my hospital room opened. A woman walked in that I assumed was my doctor.

"Glad to see you are awake, Emma. You gave us a bit of a scare," said the woman, whose nametag read Dr. Woods.

"Thank you," I replied, not quite sure what to say. "I'm glad to be awake too."

"I'm going to need to do an exam. Your blood test showed something that we need to talk about. Could you please excuse us, Mr. O'Reilly," Dr. Woods said kindly.

"Do you want me to stay, Emma?" Liam asked, concern on his face.

"I'll be okay. Can you please call Sadie and tell her I'm awake and can't wait to see her and the girls?" I said, squeezing his hand.

I was nervous about what Dr. Woods was going to say, and I really didn't want Liam there for the exam. He kissed my forehead lightly before he left the room.

"Are you feeling okay? I know you are probably in pain due to your injuries. You were beaten quite badly." Dr. Woods placed a blood pressure cuff on my arm.

"I'm definitely sore from the attack. I've also been

feeling out of sorts lately, even before the incident. I've been tired and nauseous, but I've also been under a lot of stress." I did not want to go into the details of my personal life but hoped she could shed some light on why I had been feeling so horribly. "Of course, right now I look and feel like I was run over by a truck, so I'm definitely not at my best."

Dr. Woods examined me and told me that my blood tests had shown I was severely anemic, which could account for my tiredness. What she told me next, though, took me by surprise.

"I'm actually more concerned about the anemia than I am with your injuries from your attack. Those injuries will heal quickly, believe it or not. You didn't suffer any broken bones. You may want to consider talking with someone, though. An attack like what you suffered can cause mental trauma long after the physical wounds heal. I am very concerned about the anemia, Emma. In your condition, it's important you get a good iron supplement immediately," Dr. Woods continued, writing something on my chart.

"My condition?" Not quite sure I understood her meaning.

"We were amazed that there was no damage done to the baby. We did an ultrasound when you came in, after we did a blood test and realized you were pregnant. Everything looks just fine," Dr. Woods finished.

"Baby? Pregnant? I...think there must be a...mistake. I'm not...pregnant."

"According to the ultrasound, you are. There's no question about it. You're pregnant." Dr. Woods gave me a congratulatory smile.

I sat in my hospital bed stunned. I was pregnant. I was pregnant with Liam's child. Liam and I were going to have a baby. I was trying hard to wrap my mind around this news. How had I not known that I was pregnant? It all made sense now, the nausea, tiredness, and lethargy. I had just assumed it was a result of stress. How was Liam going to take this news?

Dr. Woods finished writing on my chart and told Liam he could come back inside. He sat down next to me on the bed.

"Is everything okay? What did Dr. Woods mean about something they found in the blood test?" Liam asked, obviously concerned.

"I'm anemic. She wanted to prescribe an iron supplement." I wasn't sure whether I should drop the bombshell on him now or wait until later.

"Anemic, that can be bad, Emma. Are you going to be all right?" Liam held my hand.

"Well," I took a deep breath. "I think it should clear up in about nine months or so."

"Nine months?" Liam asked. "That's pretty specific."

"Yeah, my anemia will probably clear up about the time I have the baby. It's a pretty common thing in pregnancy." I swallowed hard as my eyes began to fill with tears.

"Baby? Emma, you're...pregnant?" Amazement filled his eyes. "How long have you known?"

"About four minutes now. That's what the doctor just told me. I had no idea. I can't believe I didn't piece it together with the way I've been feeling. I just thought it was stress." I laughed.

"We're going to have a baby. We're going to be a family. You, me, the girls, and our baby." He stood. His blue eyes sparkled with happiness. I could tell from his face he was ecstatic.

All of a sudden his face fell and his voice trailed away. He took a step back from my bed and angled his body away from me blocking his face from my view. "I'm sorry. I got carried away. I know you don't trust me, and I respect that. I won't push you to change your mind. But I do love you, Emma. I love you with all of my heart. I'm so sorry I wasn't honest with you from the beginning. That is the biggest regret of my life."

My feelings played tug-of-war inside of me. I wished I could see Liam's face, to know what he was feeling. I felt the distance between us widen. I knew it would be up to me to bridge the gap. He was putting our future in my hands. I was happy, scared, excited, nervous, and confused all at the same time. If I could get past the feelings of hurt and betrayal, I had to admit I wanted nothing more than to be a family with Liam. I still had some trouble with the idea that Liam hadn't been completely up front with me, but that was quickly being replaced by how much I loved him. He and I had created a new life together. It wasn't something I had planned, but I now knew it was exactly what I wanted.

I looked at Liam and I knew what I felt was love. This thing between us was the real deal. It didn't come along every day, and I needed to grab it and hold onto it. "I love you Liam," I said simply, looking up at him from my hospital bed.

Liam turned toward me and took a step closer. He stood before my hospital bed then slowly dropped to one knee. He took my hand in his. He reached into his pocket for something, and pulled out a ring. I gasped.

"Emma, this was my grandmother's ring. I loved her very much. She gave this to me before she died and told me to make sure that the woman I chose to give it to was worthy of my love. I've been carrying it around with me for days, hoping I could convince you to change your mind and listen to me. I know that I came into your life under false pretenses. I'm not proud of that, but I promise you that no man could ever love you more. I want to love and protect you for the rest of my life. I want you, me, the girls, and our baby to be a family." His voice quivered with emotion.

"Will you be my wife?"

I looked at this man. He was everything I had ever wanted. I couldn't imagine spending my life with anyone other than him.

"Yes, Liam, I will marry you." Tears spilled down my cheeks.

Liam slipped the ring onto my finger. Amazingly, it was a perfect fit. It was beautiful, with a square-cut center stone in an antique setting. The facets of the diamond sparkled in the light.

I looked into the eyes of the man I loved, the blue eyes that had drawn me in from the very beginning. We may not have been brought together by the best of circumstances, but that didn't matter to me anymore. I was just thankful we had found each other in this crazy, mixed-up world. Liam came to me during the investigation of my late husband. He had been trying to get to the bottom of a case that he was desperate to solve.

For me, Liam had solved a bigger problem. He had broken down my walls and showed me I could love again. He replaced my fear with courage. He made me investigate my own heart, a heart that had been full of fences and barricades; A heart that was filled with hurt and betrayal. He had taken my broken heart and mended it with his love and devotion. Liam had brought me back to life. I knew whatever the future held for us, we would face it together.

About the Author:

Heidi Renee Mason always knew she would be an author. Heidi is passionate about writing, and writes fiction, as well as poetry. In her spare time, Heidi enjoys music, genealogy, all things Celtic, and chick flicks. A native of the Midwest, Heidi now resides in the Pacific Northwest with her husband and three daughters. Investigating the Heart is Heidi's debut novel.

Acknowledgements:

Heidi Renee Mason would like to acknowledge Treena Jensen, for making me believe I could do this; Heather Jones, for your support and making me look good in my photos; Leslie Dolence, Sara Steinke, Terry Greenen, Donna Mason, Elizabeth Borromeo, and Courtney Jacques for beta-reading my manuscript. I also want to thank my wonderful family for all of their love and support.

Social Media Links:

Blog: www.heidireneemason.wordpress.com

Twitter: https://twitter.com/heidireneemason

Facebook: https://www.facebook.com/pages/Heidi-Renee-Mason/1588917641371359

Made in the USA
San Bernardino, CA
25 September 2015